MARSTON OF DUNORAN

Marston *of* Dunoran

by Joseph Sheridan Le Fanu

first published in Dublin University Magazine,
April – June 1848
under the title
"Some Account of the Latter Days of the
Hon. Richard Marston, of Dunoran"

edited and introduced by
ALBERT POWER

OBELISK HOUSE
Dublin
2015

Published in 2015 by
OBELISK HOUSE • DUBLIN • IRELAND

ISBN: 978-0-9929846-1-8

Typeset by LINDEN PUBLISHING SERVICES in 12 on 14.5 point Quadraat
Designed by SUSAN WAINE
Printed in Ireland

"God's will asserts itself progressively — by intermediate agencies — by a graduated system of cause and effect; but, in the end, and as respects the purpose to which it tends, irresistibly, omnipotently."

J. S. LE FANU

Contents

INTRODUCTION

Shadow Spawn of Secret Sin

J OSEPH SHERIDAN LE FANU is renowned as a writer of atmospheric ghost stories and novels of macabre mystery. Le Fanu's best supernatural tales are famed for their knack of establishing the spectral in a milieu of beguiling normalcy – one either contemporary with its creation or set in a recognisable, not remote past. Subtly and sneakily, the reader is enticed into a mind-wrenching wilderness of the supernaturally awful. Naught at first seems too far awry, as by graduated, discreetly distilled degrees the ominous ventures to obtrude a hoary head, until, little upon little, centre-stage comes to be held by the avatars of fright. Often, the author's crafted foreshadowings are pointed by signs banal enough, whose particular portentousness is revealed only well into the story, or on a subsequent reading; so that, tracking back along the deliciously savoured trail, the attuned reader is driven to an agog gasp – "ah! there it is: that means more than at first I thought." Where retribution treads hard on the heels of wrong, its severity is often disproportionate to the sin; or if thought consonant at all with committed crime, makes scant allowance for extenuation on the part of the malfeasant. A man may be hounded to his doom by elusive dark agencies for a murder done on the moment; but such a man may have wrested with his tempting demon, battled again and again to evade – and failed.

Of such a kind is the novella *Marston of Dunoran*, here republished in the entire for the first time since its original appearance in the Dublin University Magazine, spread across three monthly instalments from April to June of 1848. In this, the full title was given as "Some Account of the Latter Days of the Hon. Richard Marston, of Dunoran". It has to be conceded that Le Fanu demonstrated a sometime weakness for overlong and unwieldy titles. This edition adopts the running header deployed across the instalments in the Dublin University Magazine, and offers the text as a novel – *Marston of Dunoran*.

A characteristic not infrequently shown by Le Fanu is a tendency to maximise, through re-use, the uttermost potential of his material. This extends not only to themes and plots, but to the names of persons and places. Marston and Dunoran, for example, appear in other of Le Fanu's *oeuvres* and in contexts much at variance with the current story and characters. Often, too, a particular plot-line would emerge first in a short story or novella, to be worked up, maybe decades later, into the triple-decker novel which was so popular as a literary form during the middle-1800s. For some this might be seen as weakness, but most readers, I believe, would share the view of the great ghost story writer of the late-nineteenth and early-twentieth century, M.R. James, who regarded Le Fanu's practice as based on predilection rather than dearth of invention, and found "the settings of the theme so satisfactorily varied that I do not resent its recurrence."

The novella *Marston of Dunoran* shares these authorial traits, being reworked, three years later, as "The Evil Guest", which appeared as the fourth, final and longest offering in Le Fanu's *Ghost Stories and Tales of Mysteries* (1851); it was elaborated further into a full-length, three-volume novel, *A Lost Name*, in

1868, this first being serialised in *Temple Bar* magazine from May 1867 to May 1868. However, regarding the relationship among the three versions of the story – especially in the cases of the first and second – misunderstandings rather to the detriment of our author have arisen, from which the otherwise wholly supportive M.R. James is not quite free from blame.

Joseph Sheridan Le Fanu was born in Dublin in August 1814, and died there in February 1873. Though best known nowadays for his ghost stories and mystery novels, the gamut of his writing was versatile and extensive: including folksy tales of Irish country life, sundry sorts of verse that range from spirit-rousing nationalist narrative to poignant vignettes of reflection, book reviews, political sketches, and a verse-drama, *Beatrice*. Clear it is that Le Fanu enjoyed the facility of a ready pen, allied to keen intelligence and incisive, if occasional wit; but there can be no doubt that his particular genius was the stealthful nurturing of the supernatural macabre – a systematic feeding of the little black monkey that squats remorseless on the shoulder of sin-excoriated man.

Le Fanu's writing career divides into three phases. The first is exemplified by a burst of stories, with some verse, purportedly the reminiscences of an eighteenth-century Roman Catholic priest, Fr. Purcell of Drumcoolagh, which featured in the pages of the Dublin University Magazine from January 1838 to October 1840. These, together with one addition, were published in book format, posthumously, as *The Purcell Papers*, in 1880. Some of these are ghost stories, some whimsy, and some, rather longer samples, are tales of mystery and the macabre. More stories continued to flow, sporadically, but the middle part of Le Fanu's career is dominated by his two historical novels, *The Cock and Anchor* (1845) and *The Fortunes of Colonel Torlogh O'Brien* (1847). Neither of these, though well received, seems to have made an enduring impression, which perhaps put Le Fanu off novel-writing for a further fourteen years, when he returned to it with a vengeance. It is to this, arguably least fertile period, to which belong "Some Account of the Latter Days of the Hon. Richard Marston, of Dunoran" and its first reincarnation, "The Evil Guest" in *Ghost Stories and Tales of Mystery*. The sudden death of Le Fanu's young wife, Susanna, in 1858, followed by his acquiring the Dublin University Magazine in 1861, seem, separately, to have ceded the spur to the author to his most intensive and prolific bout of creativity – thirteen novels and two collections of novellas and stories, with several stand-alone ghost stories dispersed throughout literary periodicals of the time – from 1861 until his premature death, aged fifty-eight, on 7 February, 1873.

In the two hundred years since his entering this world, at least two of Le Fanu's novels have stood the test of time. These are *The House by the Churchyard* (1863) and *Uncle Silas* (1864) (dates of book publication), though *Wylder's Hand* (1864) is also esteemed as a capable, well-sustained novel of mystery. His first published novel, *The Cock and Anchor* (1845), a story of Dublin in the early 1700s, displays much skill and power, not least in the portrayal of villains, whereas most of the novels published from 1865 onwards – though each has something to offer, and several of them much – suffer, on one hand from haste of composition, and on the other from the necessity (in all but a sole certain case) of filling the triple-decker format favoured by publishers and readers.

Despite the contemporary popularity of some of his later novels, it is Le Fanu's shorter supernatural fiction which has guaranteed his lasting reputation and ensured for him a place among the pantheon of greats in this select if technically most exacting genre of creative letters. Several of his novels and one freshly compiled story collection – *The Watcher and Other Weird Stories* (1894) – were reissued in the 1890s, often accompanied by illustrations from the author's artist son, Brinsley. However, many of Le Fanu's buried treasures required more extensive digging among Victorian era periodicals, a task to which the scholarly M.R. James proved formidably adept, with the result of *Madam Crowl's Ghost and Other Tales of Mystery* in 1923. This set the pace for more comprehensive anthologies, in which transatlantic publishers and editors have been pre-eminent – as evidenced by August Derleth's two anthologies for Arkham House (1945 and 1975), E.F. Bleiler's two for Dover Books (1964 and 1975), and Jim Rockhill's three for Ash-Tree Press (2002, 2003 and 2004).

In the context of addressing Le Fanu's penchant for working up earlier fictional material into more embroidered, long-spun variants, M.R. James observed that "The Evil Guest" is "practically identical with" *Marston of Dunoran*. This assertion, shorn of inference, and applied alone to "The Evil Guest", can be defended – but only on the ground of strict and misleading literality. There is little in "The Evil Guest" that is not in *Marston of Dunoran* – very little indeed. But the reverse is not true, far from it. Therein lies the principal erroneousness derivable from James's summation, a canard blithely carried, like a smoking relay torch, with uncritical insouciance for the better part of a century, from one commentator to another, certain of whom even venture in consequence to surmise that the earlier story "became somewhat longer" in its second incarnation.

Put at its simplest there are two basic differences between *Marston of Dunoran* and "The Evil Guest". The earlier story is set in Le Fanu's native Ireland – with Dunoran, broodingly ruled by its dissolute and threadbare proprietor, Richard

Marston, serving as a kind of shadow-gloomed Castle Rackrent, in which dark deeds may with ease be imagined to abound, like toadstools under dew, and the lugubrious rackety lifestyles of the moneyless landed Irish in the years before the Act of Union fairly believed to drape all manner of evil doings in a murky *mise-en-scene* of engulfing degeneracy and decadence. Even fifty years or so on, when Le Fanu was writing, the condition of landed estates in Ireland had deteriorated rather than improved. A glance at the statute book for the year 1848 shows how critical to parliamentary concern was the easing of the fetters by which older Irish titles had become cluttered with every manner of legal impediment: the Mining Leases (Ireland) Act 1848, the Incumbered Estates Act 1848, the Tithe Rentcharges (Ireland) Act 1848, not to mention a further Incumbered Estates Act the following year and that year's Renewable Leasehold Conversion Act, which enjoyed continuing and crucial effect into the twentieth century. Ireland in the 1780s (when *Marston of Dunoran* is set) and in the 1840s (when it was written) would readily have recognised such an estate as Dunoran – a place of tangling neglect, "a paradise of bogs and bushes," lordly timbers, and tenuous cultivation. The shift of scene to the area around Chester in "The Evil Guest" and substitution of English references for Irish ones, albeit retaining the principals in their original names, make no sort of sense – especially as "The Watcher" and "The Murdered Cousin" (first and second offerings, respectively, from *Ghost Stories and Tales of Mystery*) are unabashedly acted out in Ireland.

The second obvious difference is that of length. *Marston of Dunoran* comes to just over 55,000 words. "The Evil Guest" is not much under 9,000 words *shorter* than this. Since, as we have noted, there is little in the later story that is not in the earlier (a couple of brief linking sentences), it is evident that much in *Marston of Dunoran* has been omitted from "The Evil Guest." This deficit merits some consideration.

Marston of Dunoran is presented as a tragedy in three acts – prefaced by the fifteenth verse of the first chapter from the Epistle of St. James, which effectively offers a razor-sharp synopsis of the plot: "When lust hath conceived, it bringeth forth sin; and sin, when it is finished, bringeth forth Death." In the Dublin University Magazine edition, this appears at the head of each instalment. The present edition reproduces it once only.

Dunoran is presided over by its morose master, Richard Marston, whose wife, Gertrude, he married in a burst of rash passion in youth. Over the years she has suffered severely from her husband's sustained inattention and dead affection. There is a son, Charles, studying at Cambridge, and a sixteen-year-old daughter, Rhoda. The daughter's education is undertaken at home by a beautiful governess from Rouen, Mademoiselle de Barras, who also serves as companion and confidante to the retiring Mrs. Marston. An elderly clergyman, Reverend Danvers, is a regular visitor to Dunoran – welcome to all but its acerbic owner, who yet grudgingly admires the man. Into this ill-matched ménage steps Marston's slightly older cousin, Sir Wynston Berkley, a dissolute, easy-seeming and pleasure-weathered bachelor, whom Marston suspects as having designs on his title. Not long after Berkley's arrival, a long-serving, mild-mannered servant, Merton, seeks discharge, on the basis, not that he is unhappy in his situation, or expects to secure a better, but that he is troubled in his mind by something he has heard which he fears is beginning to drive him after a fashion that he had never thought possible for him. Act One ends with a brutal night murder and the suspicious absconding of Merton.

Act Two involves the working out of the immediate aftermath of the murder: the evidence before the coroner's jury, the arresting of the believed murderer, his secret confession to the clergyman, and his death in prison. It concludes with disintegration of the household at Dunoran in consequence of a sustained, sickeningly realised betrayal.

Thus far, with minor omission, there is little to differentiate *Marston of Dunoran* from "The Evil Guest" apart from divergent locations. However, the third act involves significant departures, such that it cannot be truly alleged that the dénouement of the later version is altogether explicable from the absence of crucial details featured in the earlier. To a reader coming to this story in its full form for the first time – as is hoped to be the case of most – it would be unfair to aver too much when in large part the merit of the narrative subsists in the building of suspense. Suffice that *Marston of Dunoran* allows fuller play for the roles of the Marston children, Charles and Rhoda, and also reveals more plausible background motivation for the villainess through the introduction of the sinister and louche "Monsieur de Barras" – a character entirely absent from "The Evil Guest" and at whose hands the vulnerable Rhoda has real reason for dreading direst peril. There is also a wonderful scene in which young Charles blenches before the voicelessly exerted charms of the enchantress, so that the worst retribution that could befall her does not. In this we see a foreshadowing of the near-fatal vacillation suffered by Richard Beckett in Le Fanu's 1872 novella *The Room in the Dragon Volant*, as he is led by the amorous nose to potentially terrible doom by another French enticeress, who shares with her earlier counterpart an identical first name – Eugenie. (Interestingly, the disclosure of the siren's first name falls within that part of *Marston of Dunoran* which is omitted from "The Evil Guest".) The most obvious importance of this sizeable hiatus between the second text and the first is in seeking to understand the thrust of an anonymous letter received by Charles Marston at Cambridge. In "The Evil Guest", Charles's father hands his daughter Rhoda a missive from her brother in which the young man just alludes to this portentous communication, while not disclosing its nature. Marston reacts in fury, and nothing more is said about the letter until shortly before the final scene when Charles plans to meet his father in Chester to tell him more about it. This meeting never occurs, and the confidential mystery remains unrevealed. Quite the reverse occurs in *Marston of Dunoran*, where much of the third act involves unravelling of the intrigue and a dramatic encounter à trois at Dunoran while Richard Marston is from home, an event which doesn't take place at all in the later, shorter text.

In terms, however, of the predominating traits that drive the novella's principal character – which may or may not embody equivocations experienced on the part of our author – perhaps the most critical omission from "The Evil Guest" is a substantial chunk of the debate about religion when Marston encounters Reverend Danvers on the road while out riding. In the 1851 version, this exchange largely focuses on the clergyman's upbraiding of Marston on his turned licentious life, with Marston then venting sceptical invective against the ruses of revealed religion – but no more than by way of preliminary warm-up to his hinting at a peculiar form of horror to which he has lately become prey. In the 1848 novella, far more emphasis is placed upon Marston's openly refractory and vehement despising of traditional belief. Aghast, Dr. Danvers inquires of Richard Marston whether his rejection of revealed religion is total, or if "you confine your scepticism to one point?" Marston is unhesitating in his assertion that he dismisses all of it. Does he not even believe in God the Creator? persists Dr. Danvers piteously. Some slight relenting here, but not much.

> "I do not say in my heart there is no God; but I say, and believe, there is no such God as you describe and worship. The thing is a mass of contradictions. Take but the first, and most hacknied of the set. You tell me he is infinitely powerful. Well, suppose I assent to that, what do you tell me next? Why, that he is infinitely benevolent, too! Well, what should be the necessary practical result of both these attributes? Why, of course, that his creatures should be happy to the extent of their capabilities of happiness. And how does this inference square with the common facts of experience? Psha, my dear sir, even in these, your fundamental postulates, appear the weakness and confusion of falsehood."

By way of response, the clergyman ventures a causative explanation for the sometimes indiscernible devices of the Divinity, and tries to induce Marston to accept that there is a benevolent Maker of all things. But the tormented landowner is having none of it.

> "No, not a benevolent one," interrupted Marston, fiercely; "a malignant, or, at best, a reckless one, if you will. Why, look around you; see disease—madness—hunger—hatred. Psha, sir! seeing all these, how dare you insult common sense by calling the creator of them infinitely—that is the word—infinitely benevolent."

And then straight follows the bleak quintessence of his credo, a credo shared by many of Le Fanu's characters who have been tempted, perhaps fought, but finally fallen, and find themselves doomed – the exculpation that the sin is not their fault but rather that of the God that made them, and that they are punished more than enough by the torments they undergo as a result of it while on earth.

"If you carried with you everywhere, by day and night, a load of accumulated, and all but unendurable misery, produced by the natural working of the very elements which your Creator himself combined in your character, and of the circumstances among which he, with his own hand, plunged you—if you were such a wretch as I am—you would cease to prate of his mercy and his justice. Psha, sir; I despise this snivel, and laugh at your creed, as scornfully as he himself does."

By any reckoning, this is strong stuff – and it is largely absent from "The Evil Guest", snatches of the two men's extended exchange only at its beginning and its end being released in the shorter, more circumspect second version of the story. In *Marston of Dunoran*, this nadir of scathing scepticism is postulated, as a reader might expect, through the sinful and suffering master of Dunoran. In *A Lost Name* (the three-volume version of the story), comparable sentiments are evinced, but this time mediated in the form of reflections on the part of the unwelcome noble guest – now called Sir Roke Wycherly – who tends to dwell (if at all) on the benignity of the divine Maker as a fillip to his own unrelentingly self-indulgent and self-centred lifestyle.

Sir Roke was one of those gentlemen who utterly pooh-pooh the idea of hell. He cultivated vague ideas of his Creator's beneficence, which had been unconsciously his epicurean comfort in many an incipient qualm about futurity.

But Le Fanu is not slow to point up the fallacy of such specious comforts, in a passage that immediately follows a petulant aside vented by the peevish Sir Roke Wycherly:

Many fat good-humoured fellows smile at hell, if they do not sneer. And many bad men class it with Styx and Tartarus—a bugbear and a fable. Eating, drinking, dozing, comfortable friend! Willing to take a luxurious view of your Creator, and to make the day of judgement a good-natured sham. God is good, you say; it cannot fare so ill with us. He is the God of love and of mercy, and of every good and pleasant thing. Alas! most certainly He is also the God of every evil thing—the God of pain, of madness, and of death. Look around on the gloom of this transitory world. If here and there is a broken light of heaven, are there no glimmerings and shadows of hell? Are there not the hospitals, the madhouses, the prisons, the graveyards?

This tirade leads to a continued authorial expatiation on the logical unavoidability of everlasting hell. Those who have educated themselves into "systematic and irrevocable enmity" both to humankind and God, can never be trusted with ultimate liberty – ever – either in this life or the next. In this regard, perhaps there is a closer affinity between the first and third versions of this story than either can demonstrate to the truncated second.

Against such comparisons as these, it might be thought that the final elaboration of *Marston of Dunoran* ought to embody the acme of all merit among the three. But *A Lost Name*, though some extol its deftness of dialogue and others its felt overarching aura of ineluctable destiny, is at best a flawed masterpiece – partly because its subject matter ill bears the weight of being dragged across three volumes, and in part because somewhat of the burdened inevitability of looming fate, so constant a feature in the story's shorter forms, is not in the extended novel consistently sustained. This is perhaps less the fault of our author, than of his publisher's requirements – there is some evidence that Le Fanu felt constrained to introduce a certain leavening of mood to *A Lost Name*, which may have widened the novel's transient appeal but dampens its claim to literary immortality.

Like "The Evil Guest", *A Lost Name* transposes the characters and action from Ireland to England, but it updates the time setting from the eve of the French Revolution to 1860 and the following year. This temporal shift is manifest in references to railway stations, telegraphs, photography, agricultural emigration to Canada and Australia, and anecdotes about Crimea – together with a more evident display of egalitarianism in relations among the characters. *A Lost Name* scores, too, in positing a background in local legend for the events unfolding throughout it. This is in the person of the romantic suicide, Lady Mildred, who made away with herself, for love, in 1530, and who was reputed to be destined to be reincarnated in three subsequent generations of women, at one-hundred-and-ten-year intervals, the final one of these, haply occurring in the year of the main action of the novel, being said to portend the last extirpation of the family of Shadwell – hence *A Lost Name*. A further tell-tale sign, is a five-pointed scar on Lady Mildred's left hand – her Star of Bethlehem – which is mysteriously replicated in the left hand of Agnes Marlyn, the alluring, troubled governess of Rachel Shadwell of Raby.

Yet the deviation-free and unrelenting progress towards doom, which both the three-part structure of *Marston of Dunoran* and its narrative machinery well combine to convey, somehow eludes Le Fanu in the triple-decker novel to which this promising material was worked up. There is a little too much light among the shadows, an unmeet frequency of deployed digressions amid the gentler pastures of life, and M.R. James is not alone in decrying much in this longer work that is maudlin. In *Marston of Dunoran* (and in "The Evil Guest") the pivotal murder is very much an Act One event, with its *sequelae*, in the disintegration of the Marston family and final revelation of the terrible truth, being shunted out over a period of years. By contrast, in *A Lost Name* the murder seems to take forever to be arrived at – occurring over half-way through the book – with the dénouement a rushed, perfunctory affair. Even the apprehended killer, the admirably drawn Carmel Sherlock, is half-mad to start with, and undertakes many manic maunders before the web of grim fate is felt to close around him; so much so, that, at the last, the more tenuously drawn and self-effacing character of the servant John Merton, in the two novella versions of the story, perhaps evokes a greater share of reader sympathy, if his delineation is far vaguer. Indeed, despite M.R. James's assertion of the supremacy of Le Fanu's mode of evoking suspense over that favoured by Edgar Allan Poe, there is a much more keen sense of the American writer's cherished unity of effect in each of the shorter versions of this tale, especially the first. Dunoran may not be a place quite so claustrophobically doom-laden as the House of Usher, but its garmenture is clinging and crepe-like throughout, and the shade of its hopeless fate is unlit by a flicker of reprieve.

Ultimately, it must remain a question of judgement whether it is more apt to categorise *Marston of Dunoran* as a psychological ghost story or a tale of mystery or some kind of hybrid of the two. Since its central feature is an unresolved murder, and the bulk of the story involves its protracted working out, this novella may seem more clearly consistent with a mystery tale. But the final disclosure of truth is a result of confession rather than discovery, and the revelation itself an outcome of a systematically inflicted persecution seemingly supernatural in its incidents. Or has the one culpable fled his senses, the voice of goaded conscience breaking at last through the traces of deceit? It is an index of the skill of our author that either explanation is plausible, and each has a case to urge in its defence.

Perhaps the most helpful analogue in Le Fanu's writing lies in his slightly earlier short story "The Watcher" (published in the November 1847 issue of the Dublin University Magazine, and reprinted as the opening entry in Ghost Stories and Tales of Mystery, thereby – literally – bookending the second version of Marston of Dunoran). In this, the protagonist, Captain Barton, is persecuted by unseen footsteps on a path behind him at night; as time passes, these grow to take fearsome shape as a low-sized, ill-featured fellow who dogs Captain Barton in unlikely places at torturously calculated intervals, and writes him a threatening letter as "The Watcher". The accumulation of this tantalising tyranny, which culminates in the escape of a caged pet owl into which it is implied that, somehow, the spirit of the fiend has been transferred, results in the harrowing death of Captain Barton. Only at the end of the story are we given any possible intimation as to a reason for this systematic punishing, from which we learn that the most credible claimant to the identity of his malefactor is a man whose death some time past can be laid with fair claim to right at Barton's door. While "The Watcher" is recognisable as a ghost story because the intrusive spectral element is evidently both seen and heard, elements of just such unlikely chastisement press upon Richard Marston in the years that follow the mysterious murder. In a critical scene with his daughter Rhoda, in the final third of the novella, Marston lets the mask slip as, unwittingly, he delimns to the terrified girl the character of tormenting entity he believes has begun to harass him and is spreading scandals about him among his friends.

> "... you can't have seen him, and you probably never will; but if he *does* come here again, don't listen to him—he is half-fiend and half-idiot, and no good comes of his mouthing and muttering. Avoid him, I warn you—avoid him. ... he greatly resembles that dead villain; he has all the same grins, and

shrugs, and monkey airs, and his face and figure are like. But *he* is a grimed, ragged, wasted piece of sin, little better than a beggar—a shrunken, malignant libel on the human shape. Avoid him, I tell you—avoid him; he is steeped in lies and poison, like the very serpent that betrayed us."

In a later meeting on a travelling coach with Reverend Danvers, Marston again touches on this ghastly species of torment. This time, he describes it as occurring in a dream, which is dominated by a queer simulacrum of the man who had been murdered: "… he is the hero of the hellish illusion. At certain times, sir, it seems to me, as if he, though dead, were still invested with a sort of spurious life—going about unrecognised, except by me, in squalor and contempt—and whispering away, with thrilling slanders, my fame and life—labouring with the malignant industry of a fiend, to involve me in the meshes of that special perdition, from which alone I shrink, and to which this emissary of hell seems to have predestined me." Some small succour Marston allows himself from the recognised reality that the source of his suffering is unreal, "a monstrous and hideous extravagance—a delusion—but, after all, no more than a trick of the *imagination*—the reason, the judgment, is untouched—I cannot choose but *see* all the damned phantasmagoria—but I do not believe it real—and this is the difference between my case—and—and—*madness*." But Marston is either mad, or he is being persecuted externally – in which latter event he is *not* mad. A subsequent scene in a private lunatic asylum, to which Marston voluntarily consigns himself on condition that he can come and go as he pleases, offers illuminating pointers – but these are not conclusive. It is no small measure of the genius of our author that Marston's intensifying torments are just as much capable of being inflicted from without as from within.

From the extracts cited and the overall tenor of the

narrative, it is apparent that *Marston of Dunoran* enjoys the best of both worlds in terms of classification. It has all the twisted trappings of a tale of mystery, and is replete with the mounting mystic persecution of a great ghost story.

Akin to his best work, in *Marston of Dunoran* it is the enduring misfortune of Le Fanu's protagonist that, like an ill-buttressed coracle shattered upon lurking rocks, he is driven by inner weakness to his doom. His demons and ghosts – whether seen or invisible, and if seen however so – are, like unto each case of this author's often conscience hauntings, the grim-vestured outriders of immortality, by which retribution, however long evaded, at last inevitably overtakes, and the soul of the succumbing sinner is wrought up in ruin.

ALBERT POWER
Killiney, Dublin
January 2015

A Note on the Text

⬥

THE TEXT of *Marston of Dunoran* has been taken from its first, and thus far only, print appearance, under the title of "Some Account of the Latter Days of the Hon. Richard Marston, of Dunoran", published across three instalments in the Dublin University Magazine: April 1848, pp. 473-497; May 1848, pp. 585-607; and June 1848, pp. 728-756. The guiding principle has been to make as few changes as possible to the author's text consistently with maintaining clarity. To this end, the text has also been compared against that of "The Evil Guest" in *Ghost Stories and Tales of Mystery* (Dublin: James McGlashan, 1851). Some few errors and inconsistencies amended by Le Fanu in the later version have been incorporated; other minor errors silently corrected. Where Le Fanu has presumed to improve his language in "The Evil Guest", his first thoughts have been preferred. French phrases in direct speech have been italicised throughout. In *Marston of Dunoran*, Le Fanu tends more often than in "The Evil Guest" to employ the "pausing comma", in a manner redolent of Ann Radcliffe's *The Mysteries of Udolpho* (1794). Perhaps this can be thought appropriate having regard to the time when the action is set. ("About sixty years ago ... A few years later, France was involved in the uproar and conflagration of revolution.") Though a modest distraction, it does not tend to compromise clarity, and so has been retained. Likewise, the alternative spellings "gaol" and "jail". The spelling "dose" to describe superficial sleep (though also used in "The Evil Guest") has been converted to the more recognisable "doze". This is to avoid possible confusion arising from the later usage of "dose" as indicative of a measuring out of medicine. The principal interpolation by the editor has been to introduce line spacings to emphasise significant shifts of scene and time – a practice it is felt Le Fanu might have been inclined to, if not limited by the constraints of double-column format in the case of the Dublin University Magazine and by likely considerations of length in *Ghost Stories and Tales of Mystery* – this being also thought the most plausible explanation for the excisions made in its book appearance from the magazine version of the story. Le Fanu's haphazard use of differing numbers of laterally-sequenced asterisks to highlight *some* transitions only has been abandoned in favour of blank line spacing.

Some Account

OF THE

Latter Days

OF THE

Hon. Richard Marston,
of
Dunoran

by

J. SHERIDAN LE FANU

"When Lust hath conceived, it bringeth forth Sin: and Sin, when it is finished, bringeth forth Death."

Part I

ABOUT SIXTY YEARS AGO, and somewhat more than twenty miles from the capital of Ireland, in a southward direction, there stood a large, and, even then, an old-fashioned mansion-house. It lay in the midst of a demesne of considerable extent, and richly wooded with venerable timber; but, apart from the sombre majesty of these giant groups, and the varieties of the undulating ground on which they stood, there was little that could be deemed attractive in the place. A certain air of neglect and decay, and an indescribable gloom and melancholy, hung over it. In darkness, it seemed darker than any tract beside; when the moonlight fell upon its glades and hollows, they looked spectral and awful, with a sort of churchyard loneliness; and even when the blush of morning kissed its broad woodlands, there was a melancholy in the salute which saddened rather than cheered the heart of the beholder.

This antique, melancholy, and neglected place, we shall call, for distinctness sake, Dunoran. It was then the property of the younger son of a nobleman, once celebrated for his ability and his daring, but who had long since passed to that land where human wisdom and courage avail nought. The representative of this noble house resided at the family mansion in England, and the cadet, whose fortunes we mean to sketch in these pages, lived upon the narrow surplus of an encumbered income, in a reserved and unsocial discontent, deep among the solemn shadows of the old woods of Dunoran.

The Hon. Richard Marston was now somewhere between forty and fifty years of age—perhaps nearer the latter; he still, however, preserved, in an eminent degree, the traits of manly beauty, not the less remarkable for its unquestionably haughty and passionate character. He had married a beautiful girl, of good family, but without much money, somewhere about sixteen years before; and two children, a son and a daughter, had been the fruit of this union. The boy, Charles Marston, was at this time at Cambridge; and his sister, scarcely fifteen, was at home with her parents, and under the training of an accomplished governess, who had been recommended to them by a noble relative of Mrs. Marston. She was a native of France, but thoroughly mistress of the English language, and, except for a foreign accent, which gave a certain prettiness to all she said, she spoke it as perfectly as any native English-woman. This young Frenchwoman was eminently handsome and attractive. Expressive, dark eyes, a clear olive complexion, small even teeth, and a beautifully-dimpling smile, more perhaps than a strictly classic regularity of features, were the secrets of her unquestionable influence, at first sight, upon the fancy of every man of taste who beheld her.

Mr. Marston's fortune, never very large, had been shattered by early dissipation. Naturally of a proud and somewhat exacting temper, he acutely felt the mortifying consequences of his poverty. The want of what he felt ought to have been his position and influence in the county in which he resided, fretted and galled him; and he cherished a resentful and bitter sense of every slight, imaginary or real, to which the same fruitful source of annoyance and humiliation had exposed him. He held, therefore, but little intercourse with the surrounding gentry, and that little not of the pleasantest possible kind; for, not being himself in a condition to entertain, in that style which his own ideas of his station had led him to conceive to be but suitable, he declined, as far as was compatible with good breeding, all the proffered hospitalities of the neighbourhood; and, from his wild and neglected park, looked out upon the surrounding world in a spirit of moroseness and defiance, very unlike, indeed, to that of neighbourly good-will.

In the midst, however, of many of the annoyances attendant upon crippled means, he enjoyed a few of those shadowy indications of hereditary importance, which are more dearly prized, in proportion as the substantial accessories of wealth have disappeared. The mansion in which he dwelt was, though old-fashioned, imposing in its aspect, and upon a scale unequivocally aristocratic; its walls were hung with ancestral portraits, and he managed to maintain about him a large and tolerably respectable staff of servants. In addition to these, he had his extensive demesne, his deer-park, and his unrivalled timber, wherewith to console himself; and, in the consciousness of these possessions, he found some imperfect assuagement of those bitter feelings of suppressed scorn and resentment, which a sense of lost station and slighted importance engendered.

Mr. Marston's early habits had, unhappily, been of a kind to aggravate, rather than alleviate, the annoyances incidental to reduced means. He had been a gay man, a voluptuary, and a gambler. His vicious tastes had survived the means of their gratification. His love for his wife had been nothing more than one of those vehement and headstrong fancies, which, in self-indulgent men, sometimes result in marriage, and which seldom outlive the first few months of that life-long connexion. Mrs. Marston was a gentle, noble-minded woman. After agonies of disappointment, which none ever suspected, she had at length learned to submit, in sad and gentle acquiescence, to her fate. Those feelings, which had been the charm of her young days, were gone, and, as she bitterly felt, for ever. For them there was no recall—they could not return; and, without complaint or reproach, she yielded to what she felt was inevitable. It was impossible to look at Mrs. Marston, and not to discern, at a glance, the ruin of a surpassingly beautiful woman—a good deal wasted, pale, and chastened with a deep, untold sorrow—but still possessing the outlines, both in face and form, of that noble beauty and matchless grace, which had made her, in happier days, the admired of all observers. But equally impossible was it to converse with her, for even a minute, without hearing, in the gentle and melancholy music of her voice, the sad echoes of those griefs to which her early beauty had been sacrificed—an undying sense of lost love, and happiness departed, never to come again.

One morning, Mr. Marston had walked, as was his custom when he expected the messenger who brought from the neighbouring post-office the Dublin letters, some way down the broad, straight avenue, with its double rows of lofty trees at each side, when he encountered the nimble emissary on his return. He took the letter-bag in silence. It contained but two letters—one addressed to "Mademoiselle de Barras, chez M. Marston," and the other to himself. He took them both, dismissed the messenger, and opening that addressed to himself, read as follows, while he slowly retraced his steps towards the house:—

"DEAR RICHARD—I am a whimsical fellow, as you doubtless remember, and have lately grown, they tell me, rather hippish besides. I do not know to which infirmity I am to attribute a sudden fancy which urges me to pay you a visit, if you will admit me. To say truth, my dear Dick, I wish to see a little of Ireland, and, I will confess it, *en passant*, to see a little of *you* too. I really wish to make acquaintance with your family; and though they tell me my health is very much shaken, I must say, in self-defence, I am not a troublesome inmate. I can perfectly take care of myself, and need no nursing or caudling whatever. Will you present this, my petition, to Mrs. Marston, and report her decision thereon to me. Seriously, I know that your house may be full, or some other *contre-temps* may make it impracticable for me just now to invade you. If it be so, tell me, my dear Richard, frankly, as my movements are perfectly free, and my time all my own, so that I can arrange my visit to suit your convenience.

"Yours, &c.

"WYNSTON E. BERKLEY.

"P.S.—Direct to me at ——— Hotel, in Dublin, as I shall probably be there by the time this reaches you."

"Ill-bred and pushing as ever," quoth Mr. Marston, angrily, as he thrust the unwelcome letter into his pocket. "This fellow, wallowing in wealth, without one nearer relative on earth than I, and associated more nearly still with me by the—psha! not affection—the *recollections* of early and intimate companionship, leaves me unaided, for years of desertion and suffering, to the buffetings of the world, and the troubles of all but overwhelming pecuniary difficulties, and now, with the cool confidence of one entitled to respect and welcome, invites himself to my house. Coming here," he continued, after a gloomy pause, and still pacing slowly toward the house, "to collect amusing materials for next season's gossip—stories about the married Benedict—the bankrupt beau—the outcast tenant of an Irish wilderness;" and, as he said this, he looked at the neglected prospect before him with an eye almost of hatred. "Ay, ay, to see the nakedness of the land is he coming, but he shall be disappointed. His money may buy him a cordial welcome at an inn, but curse me if it shall purchase him a reception here."

He again opened and glanced through the letter.

"Ay, purposely put in such a way that I can't decline it without affronting him," he continued doggedly. "Well, then, he has no one to blame but himself—affronted he shall be; I shall effectually put an end to this humorous excursion. Egad, it is rather hard if a man cannot keep his poverty to himself."

Sir Wynston Berkley was a baronet of large fortune—a selfish, fashionable man, and an inveterate bachelor. He and Marston had been schoolfellows, and the violent and implacable temper of the latter had as little impressed his companion with feelings of regard, as the frivolity and selfishness of the baronet had won the esteem of his relative. As boys, they had little in common upon which to rest the basis of a friendship, or even a mutual liking. Berkley was gay, cold, and satirical; his cousin—for cousins they were—was jealous, haughty, and relentless. Their negative disinclination to one another's society, not unnaturally engendered by uncongenial and unamiable dispositions, had for a time given place to actual hostility, while the two young men were at Cambridge. In some intrigue, Marston discovered in his cousin a too-successful rival; the consequence was, a bitter and furious quarrel, which, but for the prompt and peremptory interference of friends, Marston would undoubtedly have pushed to a bloody issue. Time had, however, healed this rupture, and the young men came to regard one another with the same feelings, and eventually to re-establish the same sort of cold and indifferent intimacy which had subsisted between them before their angry collision.

Under these circumstances, whatever suspicion Marston might have felt on the receipt of the unexpected, and indeed unaccountable proposal, which had just reached him, he certainly had little reason to complain of any violation of early friendship in the neglect with which Sir Wynston had hitherto treated him. In deciding to decline his proposed visit, however, Marston had not consulted the impulses of spite or anger. He knew the baronet well; he knew that he cherished no good-will towards him, and that in the project which he had thus unexpectedly broached, whatever indirect or selfish motives might possibly be at the bottom of it, no friendly feeling had ever mingled. He was therefore resolved to avoid the trouble and the expense of a visit in all respects distasteful to him, and in a gentlemanlike way, but, at the same time, as the reader may suppose, with very little anxiety as to whether or not his gay correspondent should take offence at his reply, to decline, once for all, the proposed distinction.

With this resolution, he entered the spacious and somewhat dilapidated mansion which called him master; and entering a sitting-room, appropriated to his daughter's use, he found her there, in company with her beautiful French governess. He kissed his child, and saluted her young preceptress with formal courtesy.

"Mademoiselle," said he, "I have got a letter for you; and, Rhoda," he continued, addressing his pretty daughter, "bring this to your mother, and say, I request her to read it."

He gave her the letter he himself had just received, and the girl tripped lightly away upon her mission.

Had he narrowly scrutinized the countenance of the fair Frenchwoman, as she glanced at the direction of that which he had just placed in her hand, he might have seen certain transient, but very unmistakeable evidences of excitement and agitation. She quickly concealed the letter, however, and with a sigh, the momentary flush which it had called to her cheek subsided, and she was tranquil as usual.

Mr. Marston remained for some minutes—five, eight, or ten, we cannot say precisely—pretty much where he had stood on first entering the chamber, doubtless awaiting the return of his messenger, or the appearance of his wife. At length, however, he left the room himself to seek her; but, during his brief stay, his previous resolution had been removed. By what influence we cannot say; but removed completely it unquestionably was, and a final determination that Sir Wynston Berkley should become his guest had fixedly taken its place.

As Marston walked along the passages which led from this room, he encountered Mrs. Marston and his daughter.

"Well," said he, "you have read Wynston's letter?"

"Yes," she replied, returning it to him; "and what answer, Richard, do you purpose giving him?"

She was about to hazard a conjecture, but checked herself, remembering that even so faint an evidence of a disposition to advise might possibly be resented by her cold and imperious lord.

"I have considered it, and decided to receive him," he replied.

"Ah! I am afraid—that is, I hope—he may find our housekeeping such as he can enjoy," she said, with an involuntary expression of surprise; for she had scarcely had a doubt that her husband would have preferred evading the visit of his fine friend, under his gloomy circumstances.

"If our modest fare does not suit him," said Marston, with sullen bitterness, "he can depart as easily as he came. We, poor gentlemen, can but do our best. I have thought it over, and made up my mind."

"And how soon, my dear Richard, do you intend fixing his arrival?" she inquired, with the natural uneasiness of one upon whom, in an establishment whose pretensions considerably exceeded its resources, the perplexing cares of housekeeping devolved.

"Why, as soon as he pleases," replied he. "I suppose you can easily have his room prepared by to-morrow or next day.

I shall write by this mail, and tell him to come down at once."

Having said this in a cold, decisive way, he turned and left her, as it seemed, not caring to be teased with further questions. He took his solitary way to a distant part of his wild park, where, far from the likelihood of disturbance or intrusion, he was often wont to amuse himself for the live-long day, in the sedentary sport of shooting rabbits. And there we leave him for the present, signifying to the distant inmates of his house the industrious pursuit of his unsocial occupation, by the dropping fire which sullenly, from hour to hour, echoed from the remote woods.

Mrs. Marston issued her orders; and having set on foot all the necessary preparations for so unwonted an event as a visit of some duration to Dunoran, she betook herself to her little boudoir—the scene of many an hour of patient but bitter suffering, unseen by human eye, and unknown, except to the just Searcher of hearts, to whom belong mercy and VENGEANCE.

Mrs. Marston had but two friends to whom she had ever spoken upon the subject nearest her heart—the estrangement of her husband, a sorrow to which even time had failed to reconcile her. From her children this grief was carefully concealed. To them she never uttered the semblance of a complaint. Anything that could by possibility have reflected blame or dishonour upon their father, she would have perished rather than have allowed them so much as to suspect. The two friends who did understand her feelings, though in different degrees, were, one, a good and venerable clergyman, the Rev. Doctor Danvers, a frequent visitor and occasional guest at Dunoran, where his simple manners and unaffected benignity and tenderness of heart, had won the love of all, with the exception of its master, and commanded even his respect. The second was no other than the young French governess,

Mademoiselle de Barras, in whose ready sympathy and consolatory counsels she found no small happiness. The society of this young lady had indeed become, next to that of her daughter, her greatest comfort and pleasure.

Mademoiselle de Barras was of a noble though ruined French family, and a certain nameless elegance and dignity attested, spite of her fallen condition, the purity of her descent. She was accomplished—possessed of that fine perception and sensitiveness, and that ready power of self-adaptation to the peculiarities and moods of others, which we term tact—and was, moreover, gifted with a certain natural grace, and manners the most winning imaginable. In short, she was a fascinating companion; and when the melancholy circumstances of her own situation, and the sad history of her once rich and noble family, were taken into account, with her striking attractions of person and air, the combination of all these associations and impressions rendered her one of the most interesting persons that could well be imagined. The circumstances of Mademoiselle de Barras's history and descent seemed to warrant, on Mrs. Marston's part, a closer intimacy and confidence than usually subsists between parties mutually occupying such a relation.

Mrs. Marston had hardly established herself in this little apartment, when a light foot approached, a gentle tap was given at the door, and Mademoiselle de Barras entered.

"Ah, mademoiselle, so kind—such pretty flowers. Pray sit down," said the lady, with a sweet and grateful smile, as she took from the taper fingers of the foreigner the little bouquet which she had been at the pains to gather.

Mademoiselle sat down, and gently took the lady's hand and kissed it. A small matter will overflow a heart charged with sorrow—a chance word, a look, some little office of kindness—and so it was with mademoiselle's bouquet and gentle kiss. Mrs. Marston's heart was touched; her eyes filled with bright tears; she smiled gratefully upon her fair and humble companion, and as she smiled, her tears overflowed, and she wept in silence for some minutes.

"My poor mademoiselle," she said, at last, "you are so very, very kind."

Mademoiselle said nothing; she lowered her eyes, and pressed the poor lady's hand.

Apparently to interrupt an embarrassing silence, and to give a more cheerful tone to their little interview, the governess, in a gay tone, on a sudden said—"And so, madame, we are to have a visitor, Miss Rhoda tells me—a baronet, is he not?"

"Yes, indeed, mademoiselle—Sir Wynston Berkley, a gay London gentleman, and a cousin of Mr. Marston's," she replied.

"Ha—a cousin!" exclaimed the young lady, with a little more surprise in her tone than seemed altogether called for— "a cousin—oh, then, that is the reason of his visit. Do, pray, madame, tell me all about him—I am so much afraid of strangers, and what you call men of the world. Oh, dear Mrs. Marston, I am not worthy to be here, and he will see all that in a moment—indeed, indeed, I am afraid. Pray tell me all about him."

She said this with a simplicity which made the elder lady smile, and while mademoiselle re-adjusted the tiny flowers which formed the bouquet she had just presented to her, Mrs. Marston good-naturedly recounted to her all she knew of Sir Wynston Berkley, which, in substance, amounted to no more than we have already stated. When she concluded, the young Frenchwoman continued for some time silent, still busy with her flowers. But, suddenly, she heaved a deep sigh, and shook her head.

"You seem disquieted, mademoiselle," said Mrs. Marston, in a tone of kindness.

"I am thinking, madame," she said, still looking upon the flowers which she was adjusting, and again sighing profoundly—"I am thinking of what you said to me a week ago—alas!"

"I do not remember what it was, my good mademoiselle—nothing, I am sure, that ought to grieve you—at least nothing that was intended to have that effect," replied the lady, in a tone of gentle encouragement.

"No, not intended, madame," said the young Frenchwoman, sorrowfully.

"Well, what was it? Perhaps you misunderstood; perhaps I can explain what I said," replied Mrs. Marston, affectionately.

"Ah, madame, you think—you think I am *unlucky*," answered the young lady, slowly and faintly.

"Unlucky! Dear mademoiselle, you surprise me," rejoined her companion.

"I mean—what I mean is this, madame—you date unhappiness—if not its beginning, at least its great aggravation and increase," she answered, dejectedly, "from the time of my coming here, madame; and though I know you are too good to dislike me on that account, yet I must, in your eyes, be ever connected with calamity, and look like some ominous thing."

"Dear mademoiselle, allow no such thought to enter your mind. You do me great wrong, indeed you do," said Mrs. Marston, laying her hand upon the young lady's, kindly.

There was silence for a little time, and the elder lady resumed—"I remember now what you allude to, dear mademoiselle—the increased estrangement, the widening separation which severs me from one unutterably dear to me—the first and bitter disappointment of my life, which seems to grow more hopelessly incurable day by day."

Mrs. Marston paused, and, after a brief silence, the governess said—"I am very superstitious myself, dear madame, and I thought I must have seemed to you an inauspicious inmate—in short, unlucky—as I have said; and the thought made me very unhappy—so unhappy, that I was going to leave you, madame—I may now tell you frankly—going away; but you have set my doubts at rest, and I am quite happy again."

"Dear mademoiselle!" cried the lady tenderly, and rising, as she spake, to kiss the cheek of her humble friend; "never—never speak of this again. God knows I have too few friends on earth, to spare the kindest and tenderest among them all. No, no. You little think what comfort I have found in your warm-hearted and ready sympathy, and how dearly I prize your affection, my poor mademoiselle."

The young Frenchwoman rose, with downcast eyes, and a dimpling, happy smile; and, as Mrs. Marston drew her affectionately toward her, and kissed her, she timidly returned the embrace of her kind patroness. For a moment her graceful arms encircled her, and she whispered, "Dear madame, how happy—how very happy you make me."

Had Ithuriel touched with his spear the beautiful young woman, thus for a moment, as it seemed, lost in a trance of gratitude and love, would that angelic form have stood the test unscathed? A spectator, marking the scene, might have observed a strange gleam in her eyes—a strange expression in her face—an influence for a moment not angelic, like a shadow of some passing spirit, cross her visibly, as she leaned over the gentle lady's neck, and murmured, "Dear madame, how happy—how very happy you make me." Such a spectator, as he looked at that gentle lady, might have seen, for one dreamy moment, a lithe and painted serpent, coiled round and round, and hissing in her ear.

A few minutes more, and mademoiselle was in the solitude of her own apartment. She shut and bolted the door, and taking from her desk the letter which she had that morning received, threw herself into an armchair, and studied the document profoundly. Her actual revision and scrutiny of the letter itself was interrupted by long intervals of profound abstraction; and, after a full hour thus spent, she locked it carefully up again, and with a clear brow, and a gay smile, rejoined her pretty pupil for a walk.

We must now pass over an interval of a few days, and come at once to the arrival of Sir Wynston Berkley, which duly occurred upon the evening of the day appointed. The baronet descended from his chaise but a little time before the hour at which the little party which formed the family at Dunoran were wont to assemble for the social meal of supper. A few minutes devoted to the mysteries of the toilet, with the aid of an accomplished valet, enabled him to appear, as he conceived, without disadvantage at this domestic re-union.

Sir Wynston Berkley was a particularly gentlemanlike person. He was rather tall, and elegantly made, with gay, easy manners, and something indefinably aristocratic in his face, which, however, was a little more worn than his years would have strictly accounted for. But Sir Wynston had been a roué, and, spite of the cleverest possible making up, the ravages of excess were very traceable in the lively beau of fifty. Perfectly well dressed, and with a manner that was ease and gaiety itself, he was at home from the moment he entered the room. Of course, anything like genuine cordiality was out of the question; but Mr. Marston embraced his relative with perfect good breeding, and the baronet appeared determined to like everybody, and be pleased with everything.

He had not been five minutes in the parlour, chatting gaily with Mr. and Mrs. Marston and their pretty daughter, when Mademoiselle de Barras entered the room. As she moved towards Mrs. Marston, Sir Wynston rose, and, observing her with evident admiration, said in an under-tone, inquiringly, to Marston, who was beside him—

"And this?"

"That is Mademoiselle de Barras, my daughter's governess, and Mrs. Marston's companion," said Marston, drily.

"Ha!" said Sir Wynston—"I thought you were but three at home just now, and I was right. Your son is at Cambridge; I heard so from an old friend, Jack Manbury. Jack has his boy, there, too. D_____n me, Dick, it seems but last week that you and I were there together."

"Yes," said Marston, looking gloomily into the fire, as if he saw, in its smoke and flicker, the phantoms of murdered time and opportunity; "but I hate looking back, Wynston. The past is to me but a medley of ill-luck and worse management."

"Why, what an ungrateful dog you are!" returned Sir Wynston, gaily, turning his back upon the fire, and glancing round the spacious and handsome, though somewhat faded apartment. "I was on the point of congratulating you on the possession of the finest park and noblest demesne in Ireland, when you begin to grumble. Egad, Dick, all I can say to your complaint is, that I don't pity you, and there are dozens who may honestly envy you—that is all."

In spite of this cheering assurance, Marston remained sullenly silent. Supper, however, had now been served, and the little party assumed their places at the table.

"I am sorry, Wynston, I have no sport of any kind to offer you here," said Marston, "except, indeed, some good troutfishing, if you like it. I have three miles of excellent fishing at your command."

"My dear fellow, I am a mere cockney," rejoined Sir Wynston; "I am not a sportsman; I never tried it, and should not like to begin now. No, Dick—what I much prefer is, abundance of your fresh air, and the enjoyment of your scenery. When I was at Rouen three years ago——"

"Ha!—Rouen? Mademoiselle will feel an interest in that—it is her birth-place," interrupted Marston, glancing at the Frenchwoman.

"Yes—Rouen—ah—yes!" said mademoiselle, with very evident embarrassment.

Sir Wynston appeared for a moment a little disconcerted, too, but rallied speedily, and pursued his detail of his doings at that fair town of Normandy.

Marston knew Sir Wynston well; and he rightly calculated that whatever effect his experience of the world might have had in intensifying his selfishness or hardening his heart, it certainly could have had none in improving a character originally worthless and unfeeling. He knew, moreover, that his wealthy cousin was gifted with a great deal of that small cunning which is available for masking the little scheming of frivolous and worldly men; and that Sir Wynston never took trouble of any kind without a sufficient purpose, having its centre in his own personal gratification.

This visit greatly puzzled Marston; it gave him even a vague sense of uneasiness. Could there exist any flaw in his own title to the estate of Dunoran? He had an unpleasant, doubtful sort of remembrance of some apprehensions of this kind, when he was but a child, having been whispered in the family. Could this really be so, and could the baronet have been led to make this unexpected visit merely for the purpose of personally examining into the condition of a property of which he was about to become the legal invader? The nature of this suspicion affords, at all events, a fair gauge of Marston's estimate of his cousin's character. And as he revolved these doubts from time to time, and as the thought of Mademoiselle de Barras's transient, but unaccountable, embarrassment at the mention of Rouen by Sir Wynston— an embarrassment which the baronet himself appeared for a moment to reciprocate—flashed occasionally upon his remembrance, undefined, glimmering suspicions of another kind flickered through the darkness of his mind. He was effectually puzzled—his surmises and conjectures baffled; and he more than half repented that he had acceded to his cousin's proposal, and admitted him as an inmate in his house.

Although Sir Wynston comported himself as if he were conscious of being the very most-welcome visitor who could possibly have established himself at Dunoran, he was, doubtless, fully aware of the real feelings with which he was regarded by his host. If he had in reality an object in prolonging his stay, and wished to make the postponement of his departure the direct interest of his entertainer, he unquestionably took effectual measures for that purpose.

The little party broke up every evening at about ten o'clock, and Sir Wynston retired to his chamber at the same hour. He found little difficulty in inducing Marston to amuse him there with a quiet game of picquet. In his own room, therefore, in the luxurious ease of dressing-gown and slippers he sate at cards with his host, often until an hour or two past midnight. Sir Wynston was exorbitantly wealthy, and very reckless in expenditure. The stakes for which they played, although they gradually became in reality pretty heavy, were in his eyes a very unimportant consideration. Marston, on the other hand, was poor, and played with the eye of a lynx and the appetite of a shark. The ease and perfect good-humour with which Sir Wynston lost were not unimproved by his entertainer, who, as may readily be supposed, was not sorry to reap this golden harvest, provided without the slightest sacrifice, on his part, of pride or independence. If, indeed, he sometimes suspected that his guest was a little more anxious to lose than to win, he was also quite resolved not to perceive it, but calmly persisted in, night after night, giving Sir Wynston, as he termed it, his revenge; or, in other words, treating him to a repetition of his losses. All this was very agreeable to Marston, who began to treat his visitor with, at all events, more external cordiality and distinction than at first.

An incident, however, occurred, which disturbed these amicable relations in an unexpected way. It becomes necessary here to mention that Mademoiselle de Barras's sleeping apartment opened from a long corridor. It was *en suite* with two dressing-rooms, each opening also upon the corridor, but wholly unused and unfurnished. Some five or six other apartments also opened at either side, upon the same passage. These little local details being premised, it so happened that one day Marston, who had gone out with the intention of angling in the trout-stream which flowed through his park, though at a considerable distance from the house, having unexpectedly returned to procure some tackle which he had forgotten, was walking briskly through the corridor in question to his own apartment, when, to his surprise, the door of one of the deserted dressing-rooms, of which we have spoken, was cautiously pushed open, and Sir Wynston Berkley issued from it. Marston was almost beside him as he did so, and Sir Wynston made a motion as if about instinctively to draw back again, and at the same time the keen ear of his host distinctly caught the sound of rustling silks and a tip-toe tread hastily withdrawing from the deserted chamber. Sir Wynston looked nearly as much confused as a man of the world can look. Marston stopped short, and scanned his visitor for a moment with a very peculiar expression.

"You have caught me peeping, Dick. I am an inveterate explorer," said the baronet, with an ineffectual effort to shake off his embarrassment. "An open door in a fine old house is a temptation which——"

"That door is usually closed, and ought to be kept so," interrupted Marston, drily; "there is nothing whatever to be seen in the room but dust and cobwebs."

"Pardon me," said Sir Wynston, more easily, "you forget the view from the window."

"Ay, the view, to be sure; there is a good view from it," said Marston, with as much of his usual manner as he could resume so soon; and, at the same time, carelessly opening the door again, he walked in, accompanied by Sir Wynston, and both stood at the window together, looking out in silence upon a prospect which neither of them saw.

"Yes, I do think it is a good view," said Marston; and as he turned carelessly away, he darted a swift glance round the chamber. The door opening toward the French lady's apartment was closed, but not actually shut. This was enough; and as they left the room, Marston repeated his invitation to his guest to accompany him; but in a tone which showed that he scarcely followed the meaning of what he himself was saying.

He walked undecidedly toward his own room, then turned and went down stairs. In the hall he met his pretty child—

"Ha! Rhoda," said he, "you have not been out to-day?"

"No, papa; but it is so very fine, I think I shall go now."

"Yes; go, and mademoiselle can accompany you. Do you hear, Rhoda, mademoiselle goes with you, and you had better go at once."

A few minutes more, and Marston, from the parlour-window, beheld Rhoda and the elegant French girl walking together towards the woodlands. He watched them gloomily, himself unseen, until the crowding underwood concealed their receding figures. Then, with a sigh, he turned, and re-ascended the great staircase.

"I shall sift this mystery to the bottom," thought he. "I shall foil the conspirators, if so they be, with their own weapons—art with art—*chicane* with *chicane*—duplicity with duplicity."

He was now in the long passage which we have just spoken of, and glancing back and before him, to ascertain that no chance eye discerned him, he boldly entered mademoiselle's chamber. Her writing-desk lay upon the table. It was locked; and coolly taking it in his hands, Marston carried it into his own room, bolted his chamber-door, and taking two or three bunches of keys, he carefully tried nearly a dozen in succession, and when almost despairing of success, at last found one which fitted the lock, turned it, and opened the desk.

Sustained throughout his dishonourable task by some strong and angry passion, the sight of the open escrutoire checked and startled him for a moment. Violated privilege, invaded secrecy, base, perfidious espionage, upbraided and stigmatized him, as the intricacies of the outraged sanctuary opened upon his intrusive gaze. He felt for a moment shocked and humbled. He was impelled to lock and replace the desk where he had originally found it, without having effected his meditated treason; but this hesitation was transient; the fiery and reckless impulse which had urged him to the act, returned to enforce its consummation. With a guilty eye and eager hands, he searched the contents of this tiny repository of the fair Norman's written secrets.

"Ha! the very thing," he muttered, as he detected the identical letter which he himself had handed to Mademoiselle de Barras but a few days before. "The handwriting struck me—ill-disguised—I thought I knew it; we shall see."

He had opened the letter; it contained but a few lines: he held his breath while he read it. First he grew pale, then a shadow came over his face, and then another, and another— darker and darker—shade upon shade—as if an exhalation from the pit was momentarily blackening the air about him. He said nothing; there was but one long, gentle sigh, and in his face a mortal sternness, as he folded the letter again, replaced it, and locked the desk.

Of course, when Mademoiselle de Barras returned from her accustomed walk, she found everything in her room, to all appearance, undisturbed, and just as when she left it. While this young lady was making her toilet for the evening, and while Sir Wynston Berkley was worrying himself with conjectures as to whether Marston's evil looks, when he encountered him that morning in the passage, existed only in his own fancy, or were, in good truth, very grim and significant realities, Marston himself was striding alone through the wildest and darkest solitudes of his park, haunted by his own unholy thoughts, and, it may be, by those other evil and unearthly influences which wander, as we know, "in desert places." Darkness overtook him, and the chill of night, in these lonely tracts. In his *solitary* walk, what fearful *company* had he been keeping! As the shades of night deepened round him, the sense of the neighborhood of ill—the consciousness of the foul thoughts of which, where he was now treading, he had been for hours the sport—oppressed him with a vague and unknown terror; a certain horror of the thoughts which had been his comrades through the day, which he could not now shake off, and which clung to him with a ghastly and defiant tenacity, scared, while they half-enraged him. He stalked swiftly homewards, like a guilty man pursued.

Marston was not perfectly satisfied, though very nearly, with the evidence now in his possession. The letter, the stolen perusal of which had so agitated him that day, bore no signature; but, independently of the handwriting, which seemed, spite of the constraint of an attempted disguise, to be familiar to his eye, there existed in the matter of the letter, short as it was, certain internal evidences, which, although not actually conclusive, raised certainly, in conjunction with all the other circumstances, a powerful presumption in aid of his suspicions. He resolved, however, to sift the matter further, and to bide his time. Meanwhile, his manner must indicate no trace of his dark surmises and bitter thoughts. Deception, in its two great branches, simulation and *dissimulation*, was easy to him. His habitual reserve and gloom would divest any accidental and momentary disclosures of his inward trouble, showing itself in dark looks or sullen silence, of everything suspicious or unaccountable, which would have characterized such displays and eccentricities in another man.

His rapid and reckless ramble—a kind of physical vent for the paroxysm which had so agitated him throughout the greater part of the day—had soiled and disordered his dress, and thus had helped to give to his whole appearance a certain air of haggard wildness, which, in the privacy of his chamber, he hastened carefully and entirely to remove.

At supper, Marston was apparently in unusually good spirits. Sir Wynston and he chatted gaily and fluently upon many subjects, grave and gay. Among them the inexhaustible topic of popular superstition happened to turn up, and especially the subject of strange prophecies of the fates and fortunes of individuals, singularly fulfilled in the events of their after-life.

"By-the-bye, Dick, this is rather a nervous topic for me to discuss," said Sir Wynston.

"How so?" asked his host.

"Why, don't you remember?" urged the baronet.

"No, I don't recollect what you allude to," replied Marston, in all sincerity.

"Why, don't you remember Eton?" pursued Sir Wynston.

"Yes—to be sure," said Marston.

"*Well?*" continued his visitor.

"Well, I really don't recollect the prophecy," replied Marston.

"What! do you forget the gipsy who predicted that you were to murder *me*, Dick—eh?"

"Ah—ha, ha!" laughed Marston, with a start.

"Don't you remember it now?" urged his companion.

"Ah—why—yes—I believe I do," said Marston; "but another prophecy was running in my mind—a gipsy prediction, too. At Ascot, do you recollect the girl told me I was to be lord chancellor of England, and a duke besides."

"Well, Dick," rejoined Sir Wynston, merrily, "if both are to be fulfilled, or neither, I trust you may never sit upon the woolsack of England."

The party soon after broke up—Sir Wynston and his host, as usual, to pass some hours at picquet—and Mrs. Marston, as was her wont, to spend some time in her own boudoir, over notes and accounts, and the worrying details of housekeeping.

While thus engaged, she was disturbed by a respectful tap at her door, and an elderly servant, an Englishman, who had been for many years in the employment of Mr. Marston, presented himself.

"Well, Merton, do you want anything?" asked the lady.

"Yes, ma'am, please, I want to give warning—I wish to leave the service, ma'am;" replied he, respectfully, but doggedly.

"To leave us, Merton!" echoed his mistress, both surprised and sorry, for the man had been long her servant, and had been much liked and trusted.

"Yes, ma'am," he repeated.

"And why do you wish to do so, Merton; has anything occurred to make the place unpleasant to you?" urged the lady.

"No, ma'am—no, indeed," said he, earnestly, "I have nothing to complain of—nothing, indeed, ma'am."

"Perhaps, you think you can do better, if you leave us?" suggested his mistress.

"No, indeed, ma'am, I have no such thought," he said, and seemed on the point of bursting into tears; "but—but, somehow—ma'am, there is something come over me, lately, and I can't help, but think, if I stay here, ma'am—some—some *misfortune* will happen us all—and that is the truth, ma'am."

"This is very foolish, Merton—a mere childish fancy," replied Mrs. Marston; "you like your place, and have no better prospect before you—and now, for a mere superstitious fancy, you propose giving it up, and leaving us. No, no, Merton, you had better think the matter over—and if you still, upon reflection, prefer going away, you can then speak to your master."

"Thank you, ma'am—God bless you," said the man, withdrawing.

Mrs. Marston rang the bell for her maid, and retired to her room.

"Has anything occurred lately," she asked, "to annoy Merton?"

"No, ma'am—I don't know of anything—but, he is very changed, indeed, of late," replied the maid.

"He has not been quarrelling?" inquired she.

"Ah, no, ma'am, he never quarrels—he is very quiet, and keeps to himself always—he thinks a wonderful deal of himself," replied the servant.

"But, you said that he is much changed—did you not?" continued the lady. For there was something strangely excited and unpleasant, at times, in the man's manner, which struck Mrs. Marston, and alarmed her curiosity. He had seemed like one charged with some horrible secret—intolerable, and yet, which he dared not reveal.

"What," proceeded Mrs. Marston, "is the nature of the change of which you speak?"

"Why, ma'am, he is like one frightened, and in sorrow," she replied; "he will sit silent, and now and then shaking his head, as if he wanted to get rid of something that is teazing him, for an hour together."

"Poor man!" said she.

"And, then, when we are at meals, he will, all on a sudden, get up, and leave the table—and Jem Carney, that sleeps in the next room to him, says, that, almost as often as he looks through the little window between the two rooms, no matter what hour in the night, he sees Mr. Merton on his knees by the bedside, praying or crying, he don't know which—but, any way, he is not happy—poor man!—and that is plain enough."

"It is very strange," said the lady, after a pause; "but, I do think, and hope, after all, it will prove to have been no more than a transient, nervous depression."

"Well, ma'am, I do hope it is not his conscience that is coming against him, now," said the maid.

"We have no reason to suspect anything of the kind," said Mrs. Marston, gravely; "quite the reverse—he has been always a particularly proper man."

"Oh, indeed," responded the attendant, "goodness forbid I should say or think anything against him; but I could not help telling you my mind, ma'am, meaning no harm."

"And, how long is it since you observed this sad change in poor Merton?" persisted the lady.

"Not, indeed, to say very long, ma'am," replied the girl; "somewhere about a week, or very little more—at least, as we remarked, ma'am."

Mrs. Marston pursued her inquiries no further that night. But, although she affected to treat the matter thus lightly, it had, somehow, taken a painful hold upon her imagination, and left in her mind those undefinable and ominous sensations, which, in certain mental dispositions, seem to foreshadow the approach of unknown misfortune.

For two or three days, everything went on smoothly, and pretty much as usual. At the end of this brief interval, however, the attention of Mrs. Marston was recalled to the subject of her servant's mysterious anxiety to leave, and give up his situation. Merton again stood before her, and repeated the intimation he had already given.

"Really, Merton, this is very odd," said the lady. "You like your situation, and yet you persist in desiring to leave it. What am I to think?"

"Oh, ma'am," said he, "I am unhappy; I am tormented, ma'am. I can't tell you, ma'am—I can't, indeed, ma'am!"

"If anything weighs upon your mind, Merton, I would advise your consulting our good clergyman, Dr. Danvers," urged the lady.

The servant hung his head, and mused for a time

gloomily; and then said, decisively—"No, ma'am—no use."

"And pray, Merton, how long is it since you first entertained this desire?" asked Mrs. Marston.

"Since Sir Wynston Berkley came, ma'am," answered he.

"Has Sir Wynston annoyed you in any way?" continued she.

"Far from it, ma'am," he replied; "he is a very kind gentleman."

"Well, his *man*, then—is *he* a respectable, inoffensive person?" she inquired.

"I never met a more so," said the man, promptly, and raising his head.

"What I wish to know is, whether your desire to go is connected with Sir Wynston and his servant?" said Mrs. Marston.

The man hesitated, and shifted his position uneasily.

"You need not answer, Merton, if you don't wish it," she said, kindly.

"Why, ma'am, yes, it *has* something to say to them both," he replied, with some agitation.

"I really cannot understand this," said she.

Merton hesitated for some time, and appeared much troubled.

"It was something, ma'am—something that Sir Wynston's man said to me; and there it is out," he said at last, with an effort.

"Well, Merton," said she, "I won't press you further; but I must say, that as this communication, whatever it may be, has caused *you*, unquestionably, very great uneasiness, it seems to me but probable that it affects the safety or the interests of some person—I cannot say of whom; and, if so, there can be no doubt that it is your duty to acquaint the person or persons so involved in the disclosure, with its purport."

"Ah, ma'am, there is nothing in what I heard that could touch anybody but myself. It was nothing but what others heard, without remarking it, or thinking about it. I can't tell you any more, ma'am—but I am very unhappy, and uneasy in my mind."

As the man said this, he began to weep bitterly.

The idea that his mind was affected, now seriously occurred to Mrs. Marston, and she resolved to convey her suspicions to her husband, and to leave him to deal with the case as to him should seem good.

"Don't agitate yourself so, Merton; I shall speak to your master upon what you have said; and you may rely upon it, that no surmise to the prejudice of your character has entered my mind," said Mrs. Marston, very kindly.

"Ah, ma'am, you are too good," sobbed the poor man, vehemently. "You don't know me, ma'am; I never knew myself till lately. I am a miserable man. I am frightened at myself, ma'am—frightened terribly. Christ knows, it would be well for me I was dead this minute."

"I am very sorry for your unhappiness, Merton," said Mrs. Marston; "and, especially, that I can do nothing to alleviate it; I can but speak, as I have said, to your master, and he will give you your discharge, and manage whatever else remains to be done."

"God bless you, ma'am," said the servant, still much agitated, and left her.

Mr. Marston usually passed the early part of the day in active exercise, and she, supposing that he was, in all probability, at that moment far from the house, went to "mademoiselle's" chamber, which was at the other end of the spacious house, to confer with her in the interval upon the strange application just urged by poor Merton.

Just as she reached the door of Mademoiselle de Barras's

chamber, she heard voices within exerted in evident excitement. She stopped in amazement. They were those of her husband and mademoiselle. Startled, confounded, and amazed, she pushed open the door, and entered. Her husband was sitting—one hand clutched upon the arm of the chair he occupied, and the other extended, and clenched, as it seemed, with the emphasis of rage, upon the desk which stood upon the table. His face was darkened with the stormiest passions, and his gaze was fixed upon the Frenchwoman, who was standing with a look half-guilty, half-imploring, at a little distance.

There was something, to Mrs. Marston, so utterly unexpected, and even so shocking, in this *tableau*, that she stood for some seconds pale and breathless, and gazing with a vacant stare of fear and horror from her husband to the French girl, and from her to her husband again. The three figures in this strange group remained fixed, silent, and aghast, for several seconds. Mrs. Marston endeavoured to speak; but, though her lips moved, no sound escaped her; and, from very weakness, she sank half-fainting into a chair.

Marston rose, throwing, as he did so, a guilty and a furious glance at the young Frenchwoman, and walked a step or two toward the door; he hesitated, however, and turned, just as mademoiselle, bursting into tears, threw her arms round Mrs. Marston's neck, and passionately exclaimed—

"Protect me, madame, I implore, from the insults and suspicions of your husband."

Marston stood a little behind his wife, and he and the governess exchanged a glance of keen significance, as the latter sank, sobbing, like an injured child into its mother's embrace, upon the poor lady's tortured bosom.

"Madame, madame—he says—Mr. Marston says, I have presumed to give you advice, and to meddle, and to interfere—

that I am endeavouring to make you despise his authority. Madame, speak for me. Say, madame, have I ever done so— say, madame, am I the cause of bitterness and contumacy? Ah, *mon dieu! c'est trop*—it is too much, madame—I shall go—I must go, madame. Why, ah, why, did I stay for this?"

As she thus spoke, mademoiselle again burst into a paroxysm of weeping, and again the same significant glance was interchanged.

"Go—yes, you shall go," said Marston, striding toward the window. "I will have no whispering or conspiring in my house; I have heard of your confidences and consultations. Mrs. Marston, I meant to have done this quietly," he continued, addressing his wife; "I meant to have given Mademoiselle de Barras my opinion and her dismissal without your assistance; but it seems you wish to interpose. You are sworn friends, and never fail one another, of course, at a pinch. I take it for granted that I owe your presence at an interview which I am resolved shall be, as respects mademoiselle, a final one, to a message from that intriguing young lady—eh?"

"I have had no message, Richard," said Mrs. Marston; "I don't know—do tell me, for God's sake, what is all this about?" And as the poor lady thus spoke, her overwrought feelings found a vent in a violent flood of tears.

"Yes, madame, that is the question. I have asked him frequently what is all this anger, all these reproaches about— what have I done," interposed mademoiselle, with indignant vehemence, standing erect, and viewing Marston with a flashing eye and a flushed cheek. "Yes, I am called conspirator, meddler, *intriguante*—ah, madame, it is intolerable."

"But what have I done, Richard?" urged the poor lady, stunned and bewildered—"how have I offended you?"

"Yes, yes," continued the Frenchwoman, with angry volubility—"what has she done, that you call contumacy and disrespect? Yes, dear madame, there is the question; and if he cannot answer, is it not most cruel to call me conspirator, and spy, and intriguante, because I talk to my dear madame, who is my only friend in this place?"

"Mademoiselle de Barras, I need no declamation from you; and pardon me, Mrs. Marston, nor from you either," retorted he; "I have my information from one on whom I can rely—let that suffice. Of course you are both agreed in a story. I dare say you are ready to swear you never so much as canvassed my conduct, and my coldness and estrangement—eh? these are the words, are not they?"

"I have done you no wrong, sir—madame can tell you. Je ne le jamais faite—I am no mischief-maker; no, I never was such a thing—was I, madame?" persisted the governess—"bear witness for me."

"I have told you my mind, Mademoiselle de Barras," interrupted Marston; "I will have no altercation, if you please. I think, Mrs. Marston, we have had enough of this; may I accompany you hence?"

So saying, he took the poor lady's passive hand, and led her from the room. Mademoiselle stood in the centre of the apartment, alone, erect, with heaving breast and burning cheek—beautiful, thoughtful, guilty—the very type of the fallen angelic. We must leave her there for a time, her heart all confusion, her mind darkness; various courses before her, and as yet without resolution to choose among them—a lost spirit, borne on the eddies of the storm—fearless and self-reliant, but with no star to guide her on her dark, malign, and forlorn way.

Mrs. Marston, in her own room, reviewed the agitating scene through which she had just been so unexpectedly carried. The tremendous suspicion which, at the first disclosure of the *tableau* we have described, smote the heart and brain of the poor lady with the stun of a thunderbolt, had been, indeed, subsequently disturbed, and afterwards contradicted; but the shock of her first impression remained still upon her mind and heart. She felt still through every nerve the vibrations of that maddening terror and despair which had overcome her senses for a moment. The surprise, the shock, the horror, outlived the obliterating influence of what followed. She was in this agitation when Mademoiselle de Barras entered her chamber, resolved with all her art to second and support the success of her prompt measures in the recent critical emergency. She had come, she said, to bid her dear madame farewell, for she was resolved to go. Her own room had been invaded, that insult and reproach might be heaped upon her—how utterly unmerited, Mrs. Marston knew. She had been called by every foul name which applied to the spy and the maligner; she could not bear it. Some one had evidently been endeavouring to procure her removal, and had but too effectually succeeded. Mademoiselle was determined to go early the next morning; nothing should prevent or retard her departure; her resolution was taken. In this strain did mademoiselle run on, but in a subdued and melancholy tone, and weeping profusely.

The wild and ghastly suspicions which had for a moment flashed terribly upon the mind of Mrs. Marston, had faded away under the influences of reason and reflection, although, indeed, much painful excitement still remained, before Mademoiselle de Barras had visited her room. Marston's temper she knew but too well; it was violent, bitter, and impetuous; and though he cared little, if at all, for her, she had ever perceived that he was angrily jealous of the slightest intimacy or confidence by which any other than himself might establish an influence over her mind. That he had learned the subject of some of her most interesting conversations with mademoiselle, she could not doubt; for he had violently upbraided that young lady in her presence with having discussed it, and here now was mademoiselle herself taking refuge with her from galling affront and unjust reproach, incensed, wounded, and weeping. The whole thing was consistent; all the circumstances bore plainly in the same direction; the evidence was conclusive; and Mrs. Marston's thoughts and feelings respecting her fair young confidante, quickly found their old level, and flowed on tranquilly and sadly in their accustomed channel.

While Mademoiselle de Barras was thus, with the persevering industry of the spider, repairing the meshes which a chance breath had shattered, she would, perhaps, have been in her turn shocked and startled, could she have glanced into Marston's mind, and seen, in what was passing there, the real extent of her danger.

Marston was walking, as usual, alone, and in the most solitary region of his lonely park. One hand grasped his walking-stick, not to lean upon it, but as if it were the handle of a battle-axe; the other was buried in his bosom; his dark face looked upon the ground, and he strode onward with a slow but energetic step, which had the air of deep resolution. He found himself at last in a little churchyard, lying far among the wild forest of his demesne, and in the midst of which, covered with ivy and tufted plants, now ruddy with autumnal tints, stood the ruined walls of a little chapel. In the dilapidated vault close by, lay buried many of his ancestors, and under the little wavy hillocks of fern and nettles, slept many an humble villager. He sat down upon a worn tombstone in this lowly ruin, and with his eyes fixed upon the ground, he surrendered his spirit to the stormy and evil thoughts which he had invited. Long and motionless he sat there, while his foul fancies and schemes began to assume shape and order. The wind rushing through the ivy roused him for a moment, and as he raised his gloomy eye, it alighted accidentally upon a skull, which some wanton hand had fixed in a crevice of the wall; he averted his glance quickly, but almost as quickly refixed his gaze upon the impassive symbol of death, with an expression lowering and contemptuous, and with an angry gesture struck it down among the weeds with his stick. He left the place, and wandered on through the woods.

"Men can't control the thoughts that flit across their minds," he muttered, as he went along, "any more than they can direct the shadows of the clouds that sail above them. They come and pass, and leave no stain behind. What, then, of omens, and that wretched effigy of death? Stuff—psha! Murder, indeed! I'm incapable of murder. I have drawn my sword upon a man in fair duel; but murder! Out upon the thought—out, out upon it."

He stamped upon the ground with a pang at once of fury and horror. He walked on a little, stopped again, and folding his arms, leaned against an ancient tree.

"Mademoiselle de Barras, vous êtes une traîtresse, and you shall go. Yes, go you shall; you have deceived me, and we must part." He said this with melancholy bitterness; and, after a pause, continued—"I will have no other revenge. No; though, I dare say, she will care but little for this—very little, if at all."

"And then, as to the other person," he resumed, after a pause. "It is not the first time he has acted like a trickster. He has crossed me before, and I will choose an opportunity to tell him my mind. I won't mince matters with him either, and will not spare him one insulting syllable that he deserves. He wears a sword, and so do I; if he pleases, he may draw it; he shall have the opportunity; but, at all events, I will make it impossible for him to prolong his disgraceful visit at my house."

On reaching home and his own study, the servant, Merton, presented himself, and his master, too deeply excited to hear him then, appointed the next day for the purpose. There was no contending against Marston's peremptory will, and the man reluctantly withdrew. Here was apparently a matter of no imaginable moment—whether this menial should be discharged on that day, or on the morrow; and yet mighty things were involved in the alternative.

There was a deeper gloom than usual over the house. The servants seemed to know that something had gone wrong, and looked grave and mysterious. Marston was more than ever dark and moody. Mrs. Marston's dimmed and swollen eyes showed that she had been weeping. Mademoiselle absented herself from supper, on the plea of a bad headache. Rhoda saw that something, she knew not what, had occurred to agitate her elders, and was depressed and anxious. The old clergyman whom we have already mentioned, had called, and stayed to supper. Dr. Danvers was a man of considerable learning, strong sense, and remarkable simplicity of character. His thoughtful blue eye, and well-marked countenance, were full of gentleness and benevolence, and elevated by a certain natural dignity, of which purity and goodness, without one debasing shade of self-esteem and arrogance, were the animating spirit. Mrs. Marston loved and respected this good minister of God, and many a time had sought and found, in his gentle and earnest counsels, and in the overflowing tenderness of his sympathy, much comfort and support in the progress of her sore and protracted earthly trial. Most especially at one critical period in her history had he endeared himself to her, by interposing, and successfully, to prevent a formal separation, which (as ending for ever the one hope that cheered her on, even in the front of despair) she would probably not long have survived.

With Mr. Marston, however, he was far from being a favourite. There was that in his lofty and simple purity which abashed and silently reproached the sensual, bitter, disappointed man of the world. The angry pride of the scornful man felt its own meanness in the grand presence of a simple and humble Christian minister. And the very fact that all his habits had led him to hold such a character in contempt, made him but the more unreasonably resent the involuntary homage which its exhibition in Dr. Danvers's person invariably extorted from him. He felt in this good man's presence under a kind of irritating restraint—not, indeed, under any necessity whatever of modifying his ordinary conduct or language—but still he felt that he was in the presence of one with whom he had and could have no sympathy whatever, and yet one whom he could not help both admiring and respecting; and in these conflicting feelings were involved certain gloomy and humbling inferences about himself, which he hated, and almost feared to contemplate.

It was well, however, for the indulgence of Sir Wynston's conversational propensities, that Dr. Danvers had happened to drop in, for Marston was doggedly silent and sullen, and Mrs. Marston was herself scarcely more disposed than he to maintain her part in a conversation, so that, had it not been for the opportune arrival of the good clergyman, the supper must have been commenced with a very awkward and unsocial taciturnity.

Marston thought, and perhaps not erroneously, that Sir Wynston suspected something of the real state of affairs, and he was therefore incensed to perceive, as he thought, in his manner, very evident indications of his being in unusually good spirits. Thus disposed, the party sat down to supper.

"One of our number is missing," said Sir Wynston, affecting a slight surprise, which, perhaps, he did not feel.

"Mademoiselle de Barras—I trust she is well?" said Doctor Danvers, looking towards Marston.

"I suppose she is—I don't know," said Marston, drily, and with some embarassment.

"Why, how should *he* know," said the baronet, gaily, but with something almost imperceptibly sarcastic in his tone. "Our friend, Marston, is privileged to be as ungallant as he pleases, except where he has the happy privilege to owe allegiance; but I, a gay young bachelor of fifty, am naturally curious. I really do trust that our charming French friend is not unwell."

He addressed his inquiry to Mrs. Marston, who, with some slight confusion, replied—"No—nothing, at least, serious; merely a slight headache. I am sure she will be well enough to come down to breakfast."

"She is indeed a very charming and interesting young person," said Doctor Danvers. "There is a certain simplicity and good-nature about her, which argue a good and kind heart, and an open nature."

"Very true, indeed, doctor," observed Berkley, with the same faint, but, to Marston, exquisitely provoking approximation to sarcasm. "There is, as you say, a very charming simplicity. Don't you think so, Marston?"

Marston looked at him for a moment, but continued silent.

"Poor mademoiselle!—she is indeed a most affectionate creature," said Mrs. Marston, who felt called upon to say something.

"Come, Marston, will you contribute nothing to the

general approbation?" said Sir Wynston, who was gifted by nature with an amiable talent for teasing, which he was fond of exercising in a quiet way. "We have all, but you, said something handsome of our absent young friend."

"I never praise anybody, Wynston—not even *you*," said Marston, with an obvious sneer.

"Well, well, I must comfort myself with the belief that your silence covers a great deal of good-will, and, perhaps, a little admiration, too," answered his cousin, significantly.

"Comfort yourself in any *honest* way you will, my dear Sir Wynston," retorted Marston, with a degree of asperity, which, to all but the baronet himself, was unaccountable. "You may be right—you may be wrong; on a subject so unimportant, it matters very little which; you are at perfect liberty to practise delusions, if you will, upon *yourself*."

"By-the-bye, Mr. Marston, is not your son about to come to this country?" asked Doctor Danvers, who perceived that the altercation was becoming, on Marston's part, somewhat testy, if not positively rude.

"Yes; I expect him in a few days," replied he, with a sudden gloom.

"You have not seen him, Sir Wynston?" asked the clergyman.

"I have that pleasure yet to come," said the baronet.

"A pleasure it *is*, I do assure you," said Doctor Danvers, heartily. "He is a handsome lad, with the heart of a hero; a fine, frank, generous lad, and as merry as a lark."

"Yes, yes," interrupted Marston; "he is well enough, and has done pretty well at Cambridge. Doctor Danvers, take some wine."

It was strange, but yet mournfully true, that the praises which the good Doctor Danvers thus bestowed upon his son, were bitter to the soul of the unhappy Marston; they jarred upon his ear, and stung his heart, for his conscience converted them into so many latent insults and humiliations to himself.

"Your wine is very good, Marston. I think your clarets here are many degrees better than we can get in England," said Sir Wynston, sipping a glass of his favourite wine. "You Irish gentlemen are sad, selfish dogs; and, with all your grumbling, manage to collect the best of whatever is worth having about you."

"We sometimes succeed in collecting a pleasant party," retorted Marston, with ironical courtesy, "though we do not always command the means of entertaining them quite as we would wish."

It was the habit of Doctor Danvers, without respect of persons or places, to propose, before taking his departure from whatever domestic party he chanced to be thrown among for the evening, to read some verses from that holy book, on which his own hopes and peace were founded, and to offer up a prayer for all to the throne of grace. Marston, although he usually absented himself from such exercises, did not otherwise discourage them; but upon the present occasion, starting from a gloomy reverie, he himself was first to remind the clergyman of his customary observance. Evil thoughts loomed upon the mind of Marston, like measureless black mists upon a cold, smooth sea. They rested, grew, and darkened there; and no heaven-sent breath came silently to steal them away. Under this dread shadow, his mind lay waiting, like the DEEP, before the Spirit of God moved upon its waters—passive and awful. Why, for the first time now did religion interest him? The unseen, intangible, was even now at work within him. A dreadful power shook his very heart and soul. There was some strange, ghastly wrestling going on in his own immortal spirit—a struggle which made him faint—which he had no power to determine. He looked upon the holy influence of the good man's prayer—a prayer in which he could not join—with a dull, superstitious hope that the words, inviting better influence, though uttered by another, and with other objects, would like a spell, chase away the foul fiend that was busy with his thoughts. Marston sate, looking into the fire, with a countenance of stern gloom, upon which the wayward lights of the flickering hearth sported fitfully; while, at a distant table, Doctor Danvers sate down, and taking his well-worn Bible from his pocket, turned over its leaves, and began, in gentle but impressive tones, to read.

Sir Wynston was much too well-bred, to evince the slightest disposition to aught but the most proper and profound attention. The faintest imaginable gleam of ridicule might, perhaps, have been discerned in his features, as he leaned back in his chair, and, closing his eyes, composed himself to at least an attitude of attention. No man could submit with more patience to an inevitable bore.

In these things, then, thou hast no concern—the judgment troubles thee not—thou hast no fear of *death*, Sir Wynston Berkley; yet there is a heart beating near thee, the mysteries of which, could they glide out, and stand before thy face, would, perchance, appal thee—cold, easy man of the world. Ay, couldst thou but see with those cunning eyes of thine, but twelve brief hours into futurity, each syllable that falls from that good man's lips unheeded, would peal through thy heart and brain like maddening thunder. Hearken, hearken, Sir Wynston Berkley, perchance these are the farewell words of thy better angel—the last pleadings of despised mercy.

The party broke up. Dr. Danvers took his leave, and rode homeward, down the broad avenue, between the gigantic ranks of elm that closed it in. The full moon was rising above the distant hills—the mists lay like sleeping lakes in the laps of the hollows—and the broad demesne looked tranquil and sad under this chastened and silvery glory. The good old clergyman thought, as he pursued his way, that here at least, in a spot so beautiful and sequestered, the stormy passions and fell contentions of the outer world could scarcely penetrate. Yet, in that calm, secluded spot, and under the cold, pure light which fell so holily, what a hell was weltering and glowing! what a spectacle was that moon to go down upon!

As Sir Wynston was leaving the parlour for his own room, Marston accompanied him to the hall, and said, "I shan't play to-night, Sir Wynston."

"Ah, ha!—very particularly engaged?" suggested the baronet, with a faint, mocking smile; "well, my dear fellow, we must endeavour to make up for it to-morrow—eh?"

"I don't know that," said Marston, "and_____ In a word, there is no use, sir, in our masquerading with one another— each knows the other—each understands the other—I wish to have a word or two with you in your room to-night, where we shan't be interrupted."

Marston spoke in a fierce and grating whisper, and his countenance, more even than his accents, betrayed the intensity of his bridled fury. Sir Wynston, however, smiled upon his cousin, as if his voice had been melody, and his looks all sunshine.

"Very good, Marston, just as you please," he said, "only don't be later than one, as I shall be getting into bed about that hour."

"Perhaps, upon second thoughts, it is as well to defer what I have to say," said Marston, musingly. "Tomorrow will do as well; so, perhaps, Sir Wynston, I may not trouble you to-night."

"Just as suits you best, my dear Marston," replied the baronet, with a tranquil smile; "only don't come after the hour I have stipulated."

So saying, the baronet mounted the stairs, and made his way to his chamber. He was in excellent spirits, and in high good-humour with himself; the object of his visit to Dunoran had been, as he now flattered himself, attained. He had conducted an affair requiring the profoundest mystery in its prosecution, and the wisest *tactique* in its management, almost to a triumphant issue—he had perfectly masked his design, and completely outwitted Marston; and to a person who piqued himself upon his clever diplomacy, and vaunted that he had never yet sustained a defeat in any object which he had seriously proposed to himself, such a combination of successes was for the moment quite intoxicating.

Sir Wynston not only enjoyed his own superiority with all the vanity of a selfish nature, but he no less enjoyed with a keen and malicious relish the intense mortification which, he was well assured, Marston must experience, and all the more acutely, because of the utter impossibility, circumstanced as he was, of his taking any steps to manifest his vexation, without compromising himself in a most unpleasant way.

Animated by those amiable feelings, Sir Wynston Berkley sate down, and wrote the following short letter, addressed to Mrs. Gray, Wynston Hall:

"MRS. GRAY,—On receipt of this, have the sitting-rooms, and several bedrooms put in order, and thoroughly aired. Prepare for my use the suite of three rooms over the library and drawingroom; and have the two great wardrobes, and the cabinet in the *state* bedroom, removed into the large dressing-room which opens upon the bedroom I have named. Make everything as comfortable as possible. If anything is wanted in the way of furniture, drapery, ornament, &c., you need only write to John Skelton, Esq., Spring-garden, London, stating what is required, and he will order and send them down. You must be expeditious, as I shall probably go down to Wynston, with two or three friends, at the beginning of next month.

"WYNSTON BERKLEY.

"P.S.—I have written to direct Arkins and two or three of the other servants to go down at once. Set them all to work immediately."

He then applied himself to another letter of considerably greater length, and from which, therefore, we shall only offer a few extracts. It was addressed to John Skelton, Esq., and began as follows: —

"MY DEAR SKELTON,—You are, doubtless, surprised at my long silence, but I have had nothing very particular to say— my visit to this dull and uncomfortable place was (as you rightly surmise) not without its object—a little bit of wicked romance; the pretty demoiselle of Rouen, whom I mentioned to you more than once—la belle de Barras—was, in truth, the attraction that drew me hither; and, I think (for, as yet, she affects hesitation) I shall have no further trouble with her. She is a fine creature, and you will admit, when you have seen her, well worth taking some trouble about. She is, however, a very knowing little minx, and evidently suspects me of being a sad, fickle dog—and, as I surmise, has some plans, moreover, respecting my morose cousin, Marston—a kind of wicked Penruddock—who has carried all his London tastes into his Irish retreat, a paradise of bogs and bushes. There is, I am very confident, a liaison in that quarter. The young lady is evidently a good deal afraid of him, and insists upon such precautions in our interviews, that they have been very few, and far between, indeed. To-day, there has been a fracas of some kind. I have no doubt that Marston, poor devil, is jealous. His situation is really pitiably comic—with an intriguing mistress, a saintly wife, and a devil of a jealous temper of his own. I shall meet Mary on reaching town. Has Clavering (shabby dog!) paid his I.O.U. yet? Tell the little opera woman she had better be quiet. She ought to know me by this time—I shall do what is right—but won't submit to be bullied. If she is troublesome, snap your fingers at her, on my behalf, and leave her to her remedy. I have written to Gray, to get things at Wynston in order. She will draw upon you for what money she requires. Send down two or three of the servants, if they have not already gone. The place is very dusty and dingy, and needs a great deal of brushing and scouring. I shall see you in town very soon—by the way, their claret here is particularly good—so I ordered a prodigious supply from a Dublin house; it is consigned to you, and goes by the 'Lizard;' pay the freightage, and get Edwards to pack it; ten dozen or so may as well go down to Wynston, and send other wines in proportion. I leave details to you." . . . .

Some further directions upon other subjects followed; and having subscribed the dispatch, and addressed it to the gentlemanlike scoundrel who filled the onerous office of factotum to this profligate and exacting man of the world, Sir Wynston Berkley rang his bell, and gave the two letters into the hand of his man, with special directions to carry them *himself* in person, to the post-office in the neighbouring village, early next morning. These little matters completed, Sir Wynston stirred his fire, leaned back in his easy chair, and smiled blandly over the sunny prospect of his imaginary triumphs.

It here becomes necessary to describe, in a few words, some of the local relations of Sir Wynston's apartments. The bedchamber which he occupied opened from the long passage of which we have already spoken—and there were two other smaller apartments opening from it in train. In the further of these, which was entered from a lobby, communicating by a back stairs with the kitchen and servants' apartments, lay Sir Wynston's valet—and the intermediate chamber was fitted up as a dressing-room for the baronet himself. These circumstances it is necessary to mention, that what follows may be clearly intelligible.

While the baronet was penning these records of vicious schemes—dire waste of wealth and time—irrevocable time!—Marston paced his study in a very different frame of mind. There were a gloom and disorder in the room accordant with those of his own mind. Shelves of ancient tomes, darkened by time, and upon which the dust of years lay sleeping—dark oaken cabinets, filled with piles of deeds and papers, among which the nimble spiders were crawling—and, from the dusky walls, several stark, pale ancestors, looking down fearfully from their tarnished frames. An hour, and another hour passed—and still Marston paced this melancholy chamber, a prey to his own fell passions and dark thoughts. He was not a superstitious man, but, in the visions which haunted him, perhaps, was something which made him unusually excitable—for, he experienced a chill of absolute horror, as, standing at the farther end of the room, with his face turned towards the entrance, he beheld the door noiselessly and slowly pushed open, by a pale, thin hand, and a figure, dressed in a loose white robe, glide softly in. He stood for some seconds gazing upon this apparition, as it moved hesitatingly towards him from the dusky extremity of the large apartment, before he perceived that the form was that of Mrs. Marston.

"Hey, ha!—Mrs. Marston—what on earth has called you hither?" he asked, sternly. "You ought to have been at rest an hour ago—get to your chamber, and leave me—I have business to attend to."

"Now, dear Richard, you must forgive me," she said,

drawing near, and looking up into his haggard face with a sweet and touching look of timidity and love, "I could not rest until I saw you again—your looks have been all this night so unlike yourself—so strange and terrible—that I am afraid some great misfortune threatens you, which you fear to tell me of."

"My looks! why, curse it, must I give an account of my looks?" replied Marston, at once disconcerted and wrathful. "Misfortune! what misfortune can befall us more? No, there is nothing—nothing, I say, but your own foolish fancy—go to your room—go to sleep—my looks, indeed; psha!"

"I came to tell you, Richard, dear, that I will do, in all respects, just as you desire. If you continue to wish it, I will part with poor mademoiselle; though, indeed, Richard, I shall miss her more than you can imagine; and all your suspicions have wronged her deeply," said Mrs. Marston.

Her husband darted a sudden flashing glance of suspicious scrutiny upon her face; but its expression was frank, earnest, and noble. He was disarmed—he hung his head gloomily upon his breast, and was silent for a time. She came nearer, and laid her hand upon his arm. He looked darkly into her upturned eyes, and a feeling which had not touched his heart for many a day—an emotion of pity—transient, indeed, but vivid—revisited him. He took her hand in his, and said, in gentler terms than she had heard him use for a long time—

"No, indeed, Gertrude, you have deceived yourself; no misfortune has happened, and if I *am* gloomy, the source of all my troubles is *within*. Leave me, Gertrude, for the present. As to the other matter—the departure of Mademoiselle de Barras—we can talk of that to-morrow—*now* I cannot; so let us part. Go to your room—good night."

She was withdrawing, and he added, in a subdued tone—

"Gertrude, I am very glad you came—*very* glad. Pray for me to-night."

He had followed her a few steps toward the door, and now stopped short—turned about, and walked dejectedly back again.

"I *am* right glad she came," he muttered, as soon as he was once more alone. "Wynston is provoking and fiery, too. Were I, in my present mood, to seek a *tête-à-tête* with him, who knows what might come of it? Blood; my own heart whispers—*blood*! I'll not trust myself."

He strode to the study door, locked it, and taking out the key, shut it in the drawer of one of the cabinets.

"Now it will need more than accident or impulse to lead me to him. I cannot go, at least, without reflection—without premeditation. Avaunt, fiend! I have baffled you."

He stood in the centre of the room, crouching and scowling as he said this, and looked round with a glance half-defiant, half-fearful, as if he expected to see some dreadful form in the dusky recesses of the desolate chamber. He sate himself by the smouldering fire, in sombre and agitated ruminations. He was restless—he rose again, unbuckled his sword, which he had not loosed since evening, and threw it hastily into a corner. He looked at his watch, it was half-past twelve—he glanced at the door, and thence at the cabinet in which he had placed the key; then he turned hastily, and sate down again. He leaned his elbows on his knees, and his chin upon his clenched hand; still he was restless and excited. Once more he arose, and paced up and down. He consulted his watch again; it was now but a quarter to one.

Sir Wynston's man having received the letters, and his master's permission to retire to rest, got into his bed, and was soon beginning to doze. We have already mentioned that his and Sir Wynston's apartments were separated by a small dressing-room, so that any ordinary noise or conversation could be heard but imperfectly from one to the other. The servant, however, was startled by a sound of something falling on the floor of his master's apartment, and broken to pieces by the violence of the shock. He sate up in his bed, listened, and heard some sentences spoken vehemently, and gabbled very fast. He thought he distinguished the words "wretch" and "God;" and there was something so strange in the tone in which they were spoken, that the man got up and stole noiselessly through the dressing-room, and listened at the door.

He heard him, as he thought, walking in his slippers through the room, and making his customary arrangements previously to getting into bed. He knew that his master had a habit of speaking when alone, and concluded that the accidental breakage of some glass or chimney-ornament had elicited the volley of words he had heard. Well knowing that, except at the usual hours, or in obedience to Sir Wynston's bell, nothing more displeased his master than his presuming to enter his sleeping-apartment while he was there, the servant quietly retreated, and, perfectly satisfied that all was right, composed himself to slumber, and was soon beginning to doze again.

The fretting adventures of the night, however, were not yet over. Waking, as men sometimes do, without any ascertainable cause—without a start or an uneasy sensation —without even a disturbance of the attitude of repose, he opened his eyes, and beheld Merton, the servant of whom we have spoken, standing at a little distance from his bed. The moonlight fell in a clear flood upon this figure: the man was ghastly pale; there was a blotch of blood on his face; his hands were clasped upon something which they nearly concealed; and his eyes, fixed on the servant who had just awakened, shone in the cold light, with a wild and death-like glitter. This spectre drew close to the side of the bed, and stood for a few moments there with a look of agony and menace, which startled the newly-awakened man, who rose up aright, and said—

"Mr. Merton, Mr. Merton—in God's name, what is the matter?"

Merton recoiled at the sound of the voice; and, as he did so, dropped something on the floor, which rolled away to a distance; and he stood gazing silently and horribly upon his interrogator.

"Mr. Merton, I say, what is it?" urged the man. "Are you hurt?—your face is bloody."

Merton raised his hand to his face mechanically, and Sir Wynston's man observed that it, too, was covered with blood.

"Why, man," he said, vehemently, and actually freezing with horror, "you are all bloody—hands and face; all over blood."

"My hand is cut to the bone," said Merton, in a harsh whisper; and speaking to himself, rather than addressing the servant—"I wish it was my neck—I wish to God I bled to death."

"You have hurt your hand, Mr. Merton," repeated the man, scarce knowing what he said.

"Ay," whispered Merton, wildly drawing toward the bedside again; "who told you I hurt my hand? It is cut to the bone, sure enough."

He stooped for a moment over the bed, and then cowered down toward the floor, to search for what he had dropped.

"Why, Mr. Merton, what brings you here at this hour?" urged the man, after a pause of a few seconds. "It is drawing toward morning."

"Ay, ay," said Merton, doubtfully, and starting upright again, while he concealed in his bosom what he had been in search of. "Near morning, is it? Night and morning, it is all one to me. I believe I am going mad, by _____"

"But, what do you want?—what did you come here for at this hour?" persisted the man.

"What! ay, that is it—why, his boots and spurs, to be sure. I forgot them. His—his—Sir Wynston's boots and spurs—I forgot to take them, I say," said Merton, looking toward the dressing-room, as if about to enter it.

"Don't mind them to-night, I say; don't go in there," said the man, peremptorily, and getting out upon the floor. "I say, Mr. Merton, this is no hour to be going about, searching in the dark for boots and spurs. You'll waken the master. I can't have it, I say; go down, and let it be for to-night."

Thus speaking, in a resolute and somewhat angry under-key, the valet stood between Merton and the entrance of the dressing-room; and, signing with his hand toward the other door of the apartment, continued—

"Go down, I say, Mr. Merton—go down; you may as well quietly, for, I tell you plainly, you shall neither go a step further, nor stay here a moment longer."

The man drew his shoulders up, and made a sort of shivering moan, and clasping his hands together, shook them, as it seemed, in great agony. He then turned abruptly, and hurried from the room by the door leading to the kitchen.

"By my faith," said the servant, "I am glad he is gone. The poor chap is turning crazy, as sure as I am a living man. I'll not have him prowling about here any more, however—that I am resolved on."

In pursuance of this determination, by no means an imprudent one as it seemed, he fastened the door communicating with the lower apartments upon the inside.

He had hardly done this, when he heard a step traversing the stable-yard, which lay under the window of his apartment. He looked out, and saw Merton walking hurriedly across, and into a stable at the farther end.

Feeling no very particular curiosity about his movements, the man hurried back to his bed. Merton's eccentric conduct of late had become so generally remarked and discussed among the servants, that Sir Wynston's man was by no means surprised at the oddity of the visit he had just had; nor, after the first few moments of suspense, before the appearance of blood had been accounted for, had he entertained any suspicions whatever connected with the man's unexpected presence in the room. Merton was in the habit of coming up every night to take down Sir Wynston's boots, whenever the baronet had ridden in the course of the day; and this attention had been civilly undertaken as a proof of good-will toward the valet, whose duty this somewhat soiling and ungentlemanlike process would otherwise have been. So far, the nature of the visit was explained; and the remembrance of the friendly feeling and good offices which had been mutually inter-changed, as well as of the inoffensive habits for which Merton had earned a character for himself, speedily calmed the uneasiness, for a moment amounting to actual alarm, with which the servant had regarded his appearance.

We must now pass on to the morrow, and ask the reader's attention for a few moments to a different scene.

In contact with Dunoran, upon the northern side, and divided by a common boundary, lay a demesne, in many respects presenting a very striking contrast to its grander neighbour. It was a comparatively modern place. It could not boast the towering timber which enriched and overshadowed the vast and varied expanse of its aristocratic rival; but, if it was inferior in the advantages of antiquity, and, perhaps, also in some of those of nature, its superiority in other respects was striking and important. Dunoran was not more remarkable for its wild and neglected condition, than was Newton Park for the care and elegance with which it was kept. No one could observe the contrast, without, at the same time, divining its cause. The proprietor of the one was a man of wealth, fully commensurate with the extent and pretensions of the residence he had chosen—the owner of the other was a man of broken fortunes.

Under a green shade, which nearly met above them, a very young man, scarcely one-and-twenty, of a frank and sensible, rather than a strictly handsome countenance, was walking, side by side, with a light-haired, laughing, graceful girl, of some sixteen years. This girl, without being classically beautiful, had such an elegance and perfect symmetry of form, and such an unutterable prettiness of feature, that it would have been difficult to conceive a being more attractive. These two *friends* (for they were, in truth, no more) were taking a morning ramble together; and the gay laugh of the girl, and the more sober tones of her companion, sounded pleasantly among the arches of the green-wood. The young man was George Mervyn, the only son of the present proprietor of the place; and the girl was his orphan niece, Emily Howard. The mutual feelings of the two cousins were, as we have said, those of mere friendship, untinctured by the faintest admixture of any more romantic ingredient; and, indeed, a close observer might easily have detected this in the perfectly disengaged and honestly familiar way in which each accosted the other. As they walked on, chatting, to the great gate, which was to be the boundary of their ramble, the clank of a horse's hoofs in quick motion upon the sequestered road which ran outside it, reached them; and hardly had they heard these sounds, when a young gentleman rode briskly by, directing his look into the demesne as he passed. He had no sooner seen them, than wheeling his horse about, he rode up to the iron gate, and dismounting, threw it open, and let his horse in.

"Ha! Charles Marston, I protest!" said the young man, quickening his pace to meet his friend. "Marston, my dear fellow," he called aloud, "how glad I am to see you."

Miss Howard, on the contrary, walked rather slower than before, and blushed deeply; but as the handsome young man, with an air in which delight, tenderness, and admiration, were undisguisedly mingled, saluted her after his long absence, through her smiles and blushes, there was in her pretty face a look of such blended gratification and modesty, as made her quite beautiful.

There was another entrance into Newton Park, opening also from the same road, about half a mile further on; and Charles Marston, but too intent on prolonging the happiness of this chance meeting, made his way to lie through this. Thus the young people walked on, talking of a hundred things as they proceeded, in the fullness and joy of their hearts.

Between the fathers of the two young men, who thus walked so affectionately together, there subsisted unhappily no friendly feelings. There had been several slight disagreements between them, touching their proprietary rights, and one of these had ripened into a formal and somewhat expensive litigation, respecting a certain right of fishing claimed by each. This legal encounter had terminated in the defeat of Marston. Mervyn, however, promptly wrote to his opponent, offering him the free use of the waters for which they had thus sharply contested, and received a curt and scarcely civil reply, declining the proposed courtesy. This exhibition of resentment on Marston's part, had been followed by some rather angry collisions, where chance or duty happened to throw them together. It is but justice to say that, upon all such occasions, Marston was the aggressor. But Mervyn was a somewhat testy old gentleman, and had a certain pride of his own, which was not to be trifled with. Thus, though near neighbours, the parents of the young friends were more than strangers to each other. On Mervyn's side, however, this estrangement was unalloyed with bitterness, and simply of that kind which the great moralist would have referred to "defensive pride." It did not include any member of Marston's family, and Charles, as often as he desired it, which was, in truth, as often as his visits could escape the special notice of his father, was a welcome guest at Newton Park.

These details, respecting the mutual relation in which the two families stood, it was necessary to state, for the purpose of making what follows perfectly clear. The young people had now reached the further gate, at which they were to part. Charles Marston, with a heart beating happily in the anticipation of many a pleasant meeting, bid them farewell for the present, and in a few minutes more was riding up the broad, straight avenue, towards the gloomy mansion which closed in the hazy and sombre perspective. As he moved onward, he passed a labourer, with whose face from his childhood he had been familiar.

"How do you do, Mick?" he cried.

"At your service, sir," replied the man, uncovering, "and welcome home, sir."

There was something dark and anxious in the man's looks, which ill accorded with the welcome he spoke, and which suggested some undefined alarm.

"The master, and mistress, and Miss Rhoda—are all well?" he asked, eagerly.

"All well, sir, thank God," replied the man.

Young Marston spurred on, filled with vague apprehensions, and observing the man still leaning upon his spade, and watching his progress with the same gloomy and curious eye.

At the hall-door he met with one of the servants, booted and spurred.

"Well, Daly," he said, as he dismounted, "how are all at home?"

This man, like the former, met his smile with a troubled countenance, and stammered—"All, sir—that is, the master, and mistress, and Miss Rhoda—quite well, sir; but——"

"Well, well," said Charles, earnestly, "speak on—what is it?"

"Bad work, sir," replied the man, lowering his voice. "I am going off this minute for——"

"For what?" urged the young gentleman.

"Why, sir, for the coroner," replied he.

"The coroner—the coroner! Why, good God, what has happened?" cried Charles, aghast with horror.

"Sir Wynston," commenced the man, and hesitated.

"Well?" pursued Charles, pale and breathless.

"Sir Wynston—he—it is *he*," said the man.

"He? Sir Wynston? Is he dead, or *who* is?—who is dead?" demanded the young man, fearfully.

"Sir Wynston, sir—it is he that is dead. There is bad work, sir—very bad, I'm afeard," replied the man.

Charles did not wait to inquire further, but with a feeling of mingled horror and curiosity, entered the house.

He hurried up the stairs, and entered his mother's sitting-room. She was there, perfectly alone, and so deadly pale, that she scarcely looked like a human being. In an instant they were locked in one another's arms.

"Mother—my dear mother, you are ill," said the young man, anxiously.

"Oh, no, no, Charles, dear, but frightened—horrified;" and as she said this, the poor lady burst into tears.

"What is all this horrible affair?—something about Sir Wynston. He is dead, I know, but is it—is it suicide?" he asked.

"Oh, no, not suicide," said Mrs. Marston, greatly agitated.

"Good God!—then he is murdered," whispered the young man, growing very pale.

"Yes, Charles—horrible—dreadful! I can scarcely believe it," replied she, shuddering while she wept.

"Where is my father?" inquired the young man, after a pause.

"Why, why, Charles, darling—why do you ask for him?" she said, wildly, grasping him by the arm, as she looked into his face with a terrified expression.

"Why—why, he could tell me the particulars of this horrible tragedy," answered he, meeting her agonized look with one of alarm and surprise, "as far as they have been as yet collected. How is he, mother—is he well?"

"Oh, yes, quite well, thank God," she answered, more collectedly—"quite well, but, of course, greatly, dreadfully shocked."

"I will go to him, mother—I will see him," said he, turning towards the door.

"He has been wretchedly depressed and excited for some days," said Mrs. Marston, dejectedly, "and this dreadful occurrence will, I fear, affect him most deplorably."

The young man kissed her tenderly and affectionately, and hurried down to the library, where his father usually sat when he desired to be alone, or was engaged in business. He opened the door softly. His father was standing at one of the windows, his face haggard as from a night's watching, unkempt and unshorn, and with his hands thrust into his pockets. At the sound of the revolving door, he started, and seeing his son, first recoiled a little, with a strange, doubtful expression, and then rallying, walked quickly towards him with a smile, which had in it something still more painful.

"Charles, I am glad to see you," he said, shaking him with an agitated pressure by both hands—"Charles, this is a great calamity, and what makes it still worse, is, that the murderer has escaped; it looks badly, you know."

He fixed his gaze for a few moments upon his son, turned abruptly, and walked a little way into the room—then, in a disconcerted manner, he added, hastily turning back—"Not that it signifies to us, of course—but I would fain have justice satisfied."

"And who is the wretch—the murderer?" inquired Charles.

"Who? Why, every one knows!—that scoundrel, Merton," answered Marston, in an irritated tone—"Merton murdered him in his bed, and fled last night; he is gone—escaped—and I suspect Sir Wynston's man of being an accessory."

"Which was Sir Wynston's bedroom?" asked the young man.

"The room that old Lady _____ had—the room with the portrait of Grace Hamilton in it."

"I know—I know;" said the young man, much excited—"I should wish to see it."

"Stay," said Marston; "the door from the passage is bolted on the inside, and I have locked the other—here is the key, if you choose to go—but you must bring Hughes with you, and do not disturb anything—leave all as it is—the jury ought to see, and examine for themselves."

Charles took the key, and, accompanied by the awe-struck

servant, he made his way by the back stairs to the door opening from the dressing-room, which, as we have said, intervened between the valet's chamber and Sir Wynston's. After a momentary hesitation, Charles turned the key in the door, and stood

"In the dark chamber of white death."

The shutters lay partly open, as the valet had left them some hours before, on making the astounding discovery, which the partially-admitted light revealed. The corpse lay in the silk-embroidered dressing-gown, and other habiliments, which Sir Wynston had worn, while taking his ease in his chamber, on the preceding night. The coverlet was partially dragged over it. The mouth was gaping, and filled with clotted blood; a wide gash was also visible in the neck, under the ear—and there was a thickening pool of blood at the bedside, and quantities of blood, doubtless from other wounds, had saturated the bedclothes under the body. There lay Sir Wynston, stiffened in the attitude in which the struggle of death had left him, with his stern, stony face, and dim, terrible gaze turned up.

Charles looked breathlessly for more than a minute upon this mute and unchanging spectacle, and then silently suffered the curtain to fall back again—and stepped, with the light tread of awe, again to the door. There he turned back, and pausing for a minute, said, in a whisper, to the attendant—

"And Merton did this?"

"Troth, I'm afeard he did, sir," answered the man, gloomily.

"And has made his escape?" continued Charles.

"Yes, sir; he stole away in the night-time," replied the servant, "after the murder was done" (and he glanced fearfully toward the bed)—"God knows where he's gone."

"The villain!" muttered Charles; "but what was his motive? why did he do all this—what does it mean?"

"I don't know exactly, sir, but he was very queer for a week and more before it," replied the man; "there was something bad over him for a long time."

"It is a terrible thing," said Charles, with a profound sigh—"a terrible and shocking occurrence."

He hesitated again at the door, but his feelings had sustained a terrible revulsion at sight of the corpse, and he was no longer disposed to prosecute his purposed examination of the chamber and its contents, with a view to conjecturing the probable circumstances of the murder.

"Observe, Hughes, that I have moved nothing in the chamber from the place it occupied when we entered," he said to the servant, as they withdrew.

He locked the door, and as he passed through the hall, on his return, he encountered his father, and, restoring the key, said—"I could not stay there—I am almost sorry I have seen it—I am overpowered—what a determined, ferocious murder it was—the place is all in a pool of gore—he must have received many wounds."

"I can't say—the particulars will be elicited soon enough—those details are for the inquest—as for me, I hate such spectacles," said Marston, gloomily; "go, now, and see your sister; you will find her there."

He pointed to the small room where we have first seen her and her fair governess, and Charles obeyed the direction, and Marston proceeded himself to his wife's sitting-room.

Part II

❧

CHARLES MARSTON AND HIS FATHER parted, after the brief interview recorded in our last number, in the hall of Dunoran, upon the gloomy morning succeeding the murder of Sir Wynston. The young man, dispirited and horrified by the awful spectacle he had just contemplated, hurried to the little study occupied by his sister. Marston himself ascended, as we have said, the great staircase leading to his wife's private sitting-room.

"Mrs. Marston," he said, entering, "this is a hateful occurrence, a dreadful thing to have taken place here; I don't mean to affect *grief* which I don't feel—but, the thing is very shocking, and particularly so, as having occurred under my roof—but that cannot now be helped. I have resolved to spare no exertions, and no influence, to bring the assassin to justice—and a coroner's jury will, within a few hours, sift the evidence which we have succeeded in collecting—but, my purpose in seeking you now is, to recur to the conversation we yesterday had, respecting a member of this establishment."

"Mademoiselle de Barras?" suggested the lady.

"Yes, Mademoiselle de Barras," echoed Marston; "I wish to say, that, having reconsidered the circumstances affecting her, I am absolutely resolved that she shall not continue to be an inmate of this house."

He paused—and Mrs. Marston said—"Well, Richard, I am sorry, very sorry for it; but your decision shall never be disputed by me."

"Of course," said Marston, drily; "and, therefore, the

sooner you acquaint her with it, and let her know that she must go, the better."

Having said this, he left her, and went to his own chamber, where he proceeded to make his toilet with elaborate propriety, in preparation for the scene which was about to take place under his roof.

Mrs. Marston, meanwhile, suffered from a horrible uncertainty. She never harboured, it is true, one doubt as to her husband's perfect innocence of the ghastly crime which filled their house with fear and gloom; but, at the same time that she thoroughly and indignantly scouted the possibility of his, under any circumstances, being accessory to such a crime, she experienced a nervous and agonizing anxiety lest any one else should possibly suspect him, however obliquely and faintly, of any participation whatever in the foul deed. This vague fear tortured her—it had taken possession of her mind; and it was the more acutely painful, because it was of a kind which precluded the possibility of her dispelling it, as morbid fears so often are dispelled, by taking counsel upon its suggestions with a friend.

The day wore on, and strange faces began to fill the great parlour. The coroner, accompanied by a physician, had arrived. Several of the gentry in the immediate vicinity had been summoned as jurors, and now began to arrive in succession. Marston, in a handsome and sober suit, received these visitors with a stately and melancholy courtesy, befitting the occasion. Mervyn and his son had both been summoned, and, of course, were in attendance. There being now a sufficient number to form a jury, they were sworn, and immediately proceeded to the chamber where the body of the murdered man was lying.

Marston accompanied them, and with a pale and stern countenance, and in a clear and subdued tone, called their attention successively to every particular detail which he conceived important to be noted. Having thus employed some minutes, the jury again returned to the parlour, and the examination of the witnesses commenced.

Marston, at his own request, was first sworn and examined. He deposed merely to the circumstance of his parting, on the night previous, with Sir Wynston, and to the state in which he had seen the room and the body in the morning. He mentioned also the fact, that on hearing the alarm in the morning, he had hastened from his own chamber to Sir Wynston's, and found, on trying to enter, that the door opening upon the passage was secured on the inside. This circumstance shewed that the murderer must have made his egress at least through the valet's chamber, and by the back-stairs. Marston's evidence went no further.

The next witness sworn was Edward Smith, the servant of the late Sir Wynston Berkley. His evidence was a narrative of the occurrences we have already stated. He described the sounds which he had overheard from his master's room, the subsequent appearance of Merton, and the conversation which had passed between them. He then proceeded to mention, that it was his master's custom to have himself called at seven o'clock, at which hour he usually took some medicine, which it was the valet's duty to bring to him; after which he either settled again to rest, or rose in a short time, if unable to sleep. Having measured and prepared this dose in the dressing-room, the servant went on to say, he had knocked at his master's door, and receiving no answer, had entered the room, and partly unclosed the shutters. He perceived the blood on the carpet, and on opening the curtains, saw his master lying with his mouth and eyes open, perfectly dead, and weltering in gore. He had stretched out his hand, and seized that of the dead man, which was quite stiff and cold;

then, losing heart, he had run to the door communicating with the passage, but found it locked, and turned to the other entrance, and ran down the back-stairs, crying "murder." Mr. Hughes, the butler, and James Carney, another servant, came immediately, and they all three went back into the room. The key was in the outer door, upon the inside, but they did not unlock it until they had viewed the body. There was a great pool of blood in the bed, and in it was lying a red-handled case-knife, which was produced, and identified by the witness. Just then they heard Mr. Marston calling for admission, and they opened the door with some difficulty, for the lock was rusty. Mr. Marston had then ordered them to leave the things as they were, and had used very stern language to the witness. They had then left the room, securing both doors.

This witness underwent a severe and searching examination, but his evidence was clear and consistent.

In conclusion, Marston produced a dagger, which was stained with blood, and asked the man whether he recognised it.

Smith at once stated this to have been the property of his late master, who, when travelling, carried it, together with his pistols, along with him. Since his arrival at Dunoran, it had lain upon the chimney-piece in his bedroom, where he believed it to have been upon the previous night.

James Carney, one of Marston's servants, was next sworn and examined. He had, he said, observed a strange and unaccountable agitation and depression in Merton's manner for some days past; he had also been several times disturbed at night by his talking aloud to himself, and walking to and fro in his room. Their bedrooms were separated by a thin partition, in which was a window, through which Carney had, on the night of the murder, observed a light in Merton's room, and, on looking in, had seen him dressing hastily. He also saw him twice take up, and again lay down, the red-hafted knife which had been found in the bed of the murdered man. He knew it by the handle being broken near the end. He had no suspicion of Merton having any mischievous intentions, and lay down again to rest. He afterwards heard him pass out of his room, and go slowly up the back-stairs leading to the upper story. Shortly after this he had fallen asleep, and did not hear or see him return. He then described, as Smith had already done, the scene which presented itself in the morning, on his accompanying him into Sir Wynston's bedchamber.

The next witness examined was a little boy, who described himself as "a poor scholar." His testimony was somewhat singular. He deposed that he had come to the house on the preceding evening, and had been given some supper, and was afterwards permitted to sleep among the hay in one of the lofts. He had, however, discovered what he considered a snugger berth. This was an unused stable, in the further end of which lay a quantity of hay. Among this he had lain down, and gone to sleep. He was, however, awakened in the course of the night, by the entrance of a man, whom he saw with perfect distinctness in the moonlight, and his description of his dress and appearance tallied exactly with those of Merton. This man occupied himself for some time in washing his hands and face in a stable bucket, which happened to stand by the door; and, during the whole of this process, he continued to moan and mutter like one in woful perturbation. He said, distinctly, twice or thrice, "by _____, I am done for;" and every now and then he muttered, "and nothing for it, after all." When he had done washing his hands, he took something from his coat-pocket, and looked at it, shaking his head; at this time he was standing with his back turned toward the boy, so that he could not see what this object might be. The man, however, put it into his breast, and then began to search hurriedly, as it seemed, for some hiding-place for it. After looking at the pavement, and poking at the chinks of the wall, he suddenly went to the window, and forced up the stone which formed the sill; under this he threw the object which the boy had seen him examine with so much perplexity, and then he re-adjusted the stone, and removed the evidences of its having been recently stirred. The boy was a little frightened, but very curious at all that he saw; and when the man left the stable in which he lay, he got up, and following to the door, peeped after him. He saw him putting on an outside-coat and hat, near the yard gate; and then, with great caution, unbolt the wicket, constantly looking back towards the house; and so, let himself out. The boy was uneasy, and sat in the hay, wide awake, until morning. He then told the servants what he had seen, and one of the men having raised the stone, which *he* had not strength to lift, they found the dagger which Smith had identified as belonging to his master. This weapon was stained with blood; and some hair, which was found to correspond in colour with Sir Wynston's, was sticking in the crevice between the blade and the handle.

"It appears very strange that *one* man should have employed two distinct instruments of this kind," observed Mervyn, after a pause. A silence followed.

"Yes, strange; it *does* seem strange," said Marston, clearing his voice.

"Yet, it is clear," said another of the jury, "that the same hand *did* employ them—it is proved that the knife was in Merton's possession just as he left his chamber, and proved also that the dagger was secreted by him, after he quitted the house."

"Yes," said Marston, with a grizly sort of smile, and glancing sarcastically at Mervyn, while he addressed the last speaker—"I thank you for recalling my attention to the facts—

it certainly is not a very pleasant suggestion, that there still remains within my household an undetected murderer."

Mervyn ruminated for a time, and said he should wish to put a few more questions to Smith and Carney. They were accordingly recalled, and examined in great detail, with a view to ascertain whether any indication of the presence of a second person having visited the chamber with Merton was discoverable. Nothing, however, appeared, except that the valet mentioned the noise and the exclamations which he had indistinctly heard.

"You did not mention that before, sir," said Marston, sharply.

"I did not think of it, sir," replied the man, "the gentlemen were asking me so many questions; but I told you, sir, about it in the morning."

"Oh, ah—yes, yes—I believe you did," said Marston; "but you then said that Sir Wynston often talked when he was alone—eh, sir?"

"Yes, sir, and so he used, which was the reason I did not go into the room when I heard it," replied the man.

"How long afterwards was it when you saw Merton in your own room?" asked Mervyn.

"I could not say, sir," answered Smith; "I was soon asleep, and can't say how long I slept before he came."

"Was it an hour?" pursued Mervyn.

"I can't say," said the man, doubtfully.

"Was it five hours?" asked Marston.

"No, sir; I am sure it was not five."

"Could you swear it was more than half-an-hour?" persisted Marston.

"No, I could not swear that," answered he.

"I am afraid, Mr. Mervyn, you have found a mare's nest," said Marston, contemptuously.

"I have done my duty, sir," retorted Mervyn, cynically; "which plainly requires that I shall leave no doubt which the evidence of the witnesses can clear up, unsifted and unsatisfied. I happened to think it of some moment to ascertain, if possible, whether more persons than one were engaged in this atrocious murder—you don't seem to think the question so important a one—different men, sir, take different views."

"Views, sir, in matters of this sort, especially where they tend to multiply suspicions, and to implicate others, ought to be supported by something more substantial than mere fancies," retorted Marston.

"I don't know what you call fancies," replied Mervyn, testily, "but, here are *two* deadly weapons, a knife and a dagger—each, it would seem, employed in doing this murder—if you see nothing odd in that, I can't enable you to do so."

"Well, sir," said Marston, grimly, "the *whole* thing is, as you term it, *odd*, and I can see no object in your picking out this particular singularity for long-winded criticism, except to cast scandal upon my household, by leaving a hideous and vague imputation floating among the members of it. Sir—sir—this is a foul way," he cried sternly, "to gratify a paltry spite."

"Mr. Marston," said Mervyn, rising and thrusting his hands into his pockets, while he confronted him to the full as sternly, "the country knows in which of our hearts the spite, if any there is between us, is harboured. I owe you no friendship—but, sir, I cherish no malice either; and against the worst enemy I have on earth I am incapable of perverting an opportunity like this, and inflicting pain, under the pretence of discharging a duty."

Marston was on the point of interrupting, but the coroner interposed, and besought them to confine their attention strictly to the solemn inquiry which they were summoned together to prosecute. Meanwhile George Mervyn and Charles Marston were deeply pained and embarrassed at this fiery renewal of mutual hostilities between their parents; at a moment, too, when each had cherished the hope that they would, at least upon this occasion, have met without the exhibition of angry feelings.

There remained still to be examined the surgeon who had accompanied the coroner, for the purpose of reporting upon the extent and nature of the injuries discoverable upon the person of the deceased. He accordingly deposed, that having examined the body, he found no less than five deep wounds, inflicted with some sharp instrument; two of them had actually penetrated the heart, and had, of course, caused instant death. Besides these, there were two contusions, one upon the back of the head, the other upon the forehead, with a slight abrasion of the eyebrow. There was a large lock of hair torn out by the roots at the front of the head, and the palm and fingers of the right hand were cut. This evidence having been taken, the jury once more repaired to the chamber where the body lay, and proceeded with much minuteness to examine the room, with a view to ascertain, if possible, more particularly, the exact circumstances of the murder.

The result of this elaborate scrutiny was as follows: The deceased, they conjectured, had fallen asleep in his easy chair, and, while he was unconscious, the murderer had stolen into the room, and, before attacking his victim, had secured the bedroom door upon the inside—this was argued from the non-discovery of blood upon the handle, or any other part of the door. It was supposed that he had then approached Sir Wynston, with the view either of robbing, or of murdering him while he slept, and that the deceased had awakened just after he had reached him—that a brief and desperate struggle had ensued, in which the assailant had struck his victim with his fist upon the forehead, and having stunned him, had hurriedly clutched him by the hair, and stabbed him with the dagger which lay close by upon the chimney-piece, forcing his head violently against the back of the chair. This part of the conjecture was supported by the circumstance of there being discovered a lock of hair upon the ground, at the spot, and a good deal of blood. The carpet, too, was tossed, and a water-croft which had stood upon the table close by, was lying in fragments upon the floor. It was supposed that the murderer had then dragged the half-lifeless body to the bed, where, having substituted the knife, which he had probably brought to the room in the same pocket from which the boy afterwards saw him take the dagger, he dispatched him; and either hearing some alarm—perhaps the movement of the valet in the adjoining room, or from some other cause—he dropped the knife in the bed, and was not able to find it again. The wounds upon the hand of the dead man indicated his having caught and struggled to hold the blade of the weapon with which he was assailed. The impression of a bloody hand thrust under the bolster, where it was Sir Wynston's habit to place his purse and watch, when making his arrangements for the night, supplied the motive of this otherwise unaccountable atrocity.

After some brief consultation, the jury agreed upon a verdict of wilful murder against John Merton, a finding of which the coroner expressed his entire approbation.

As the two young friends, George Mervyn and Charles, passed through the hall, they saw Rhoda gliding into her little study. Mervyn hesitated, as if about to follow her; but sighed, and said, after a moment's pause—"Charles, I think she is more beautiful than ever."

Charles looked gratified, and replied—"She is greatly

improved since I saw her last—she is certainly *very* pretty."

They walked on in silence, and after a few seconds, Mervyn said, with a sigh—"You can't think how my father's unhappy disagreement with yours afflicts me. I could have died with vexation to-day."

"It is, indeed, a deplorable thing—such near neighbours, too," replied Charles.

It was quite plain in what direction the thoughts of the two young men were travelling.

Marston, as a justice of the peace, had informations, embodying the principal part of the evidence given before the coroner, sworn against Merton, and transmitted a copy of them to the castle. A reward for the apprehension of the culprit was forthwith offered in the *Gazette*, but for some months without effect.

Marston had, in the interval, written to several of Sir Wynston's many relations announcing the catastrophe, and requesting that steps might immediately be taken to have the body removed. Meanwhile, undertakers were busy in the chamber of death. The corpse was inclosed in lead, and that again in cedar, and a great oak shell, covered with crimson cloth and gold-headed nails, and with a gilt plate recording the age, title, &c. &c., was screwed down firmly over all.

Nearly three weeks elapsed before any reply to Marston's letters was received. A short epistle at last arrived from Lord H_____, the late Sir Wynston's uncle, deeply regretting "the sad and inexplicable occurrence;" and adding, that the will which, on receipt of the "distressing intelligence," was immediately opened and read, contained no direction whatever respecting the sepulture of the deceased, which had therefore better be completed as modestly and expeditiously as possible, in the neighbourhood of Dunoran; and, in conclusion, he directed that the accounts of the undertakers, &c., employed upon the melancholy occasion, might be sent in to Mr. Skelton, who had kindly undertaken to leave London for Ireland without any delay, for the purpose of completing these last arrangements, and who would, in any matter of business connected with the deceased, represent him, Lord H_____, as executor of the late baronet.

This letter was followed, in a day or two, by the arrival of Skelton—a well-dressed, languid, impertinent London tuft-hunter—a good deal faded—with a somewhat sallow and puffy face, charged with a pleasant combination at once of meanness, insolence, and sensuality—just such a person as Sir Wynston's parasite might have been expected to prove.

However well disposed to impress the natives of Dunoran with high notions of his extraordinary refinement and importance, he very soon discovered, that, in Marston, he had stumbled upon a man of the world, and one thoroughly versed in the ways and characters of London life. After some ineffectual attempts, therefore, to overawe and astonish his host, Mr. Skelton became aware of the fruitlessness of the effort, and condescended to abate somewhat of his pretensions.

Marston could not avoid inviting this person to pass the night at Dunoran, an invitation which was accepted, of course; and next morning, after a late breakfast, Mr. Skelton observed, with a yawn—

"And now, about this body—poor Berkley!—what do you propose to do with him?"

"I have no proposition to make," said Marston, drily; "it is no affair of mine, except that the body may be removed without more delay. I have no suggestion to offer."

"H_____'s notion was to have him buried as near the spot as may be," said Skelton.

Marston nodded.

"There is a kind of vault—is there not—in the demesne, a family burial place?" inquired his visitor.

"Yes, sir," replied Marston, curtly.

"Well?" drawled Skelton.

"Well, sir; what then?" responded Marston.

"Why, as the wish of the parties is to have him buried—poor fellow!—as quietly as possible, I think he might just as well be laid *there* as anywhere else."

"Had I desired it, Mr. Skelton, I should myself have made the offer," said Marston, abruptly.

"Then you don't wish it?" said Skelton.

"No, sir; certainly not—most peremptorily not," answered Marston, with more sharpness than, in his early days, he would have thought quite consistent with politeness.

"Perhaps," replied Skelton, for want of something better to say, and with a callous sort of levity—"perhaps you hold the idea—some people *do*—that murdered men can't rest in their graves until their murderers have expiated their guilt?"

Marston made no reply, but shot two or three livid glances from under his brow, at the speaker.

"Well, then, at all events," continued Skelton, indolently resuming his theme, "if you decline your assistance, may I, at least, hope for your advice? Knowing nothing of this country, I would ask you whither you would recommend me to have the body conveyed?"

"I don't care to advise in the matter," said Marston, "but if I were directing, I should have the remains buried in the city of Dublin. It is not more than twenty miles from this; and if at any future time his family should desire to remove the body to England, it could be effected more easily from thence. But you can decide."

"Egad! I believe you are right," said Skelton, glad to be

relieved of the trouble of thinking about the matter; "and I shall take your advice."

In accordance with this declaration, the body was, within four-and-twenty hours, removed to Dublin, and buried there in St. Peter's churchyard, Mr. Skelton attending on behalf of Sir Wynston's numerous and afflicted friends and relatives.

There are certain heartaches for which time brings no healing; nay, which grow but the sorer and fiercer as days and years roll on. Of this kind, perhaps, was the stern and bitter feeling which now darkened the face of Marston, with an almost perpetual gloom. His habits became even more unsocial than before. The society of his son he no longer seemed to enjoy. Long and solitary rambles in his wild and extensive demesne consumed the listless hours of his waking existence; and when the weather prevented this, he shut himself up, upon pretence of business, in his study.

He had not, since the occasion we have already mentioned, referred to the intended departure of Mademoiselle de Barras. Truth to say, his feelings with respect to that young lady were of a conflicting and mysterious kind; and as often as his dark thoughts wandered to her (which indeed was frequently enough), his muttered exclamations seemed to imply some painful and horrible suspicions respecting her.

"Yes," he would mutter, "I thought I heard your light foot upon the lobby, on that *accursed* night. *Fancy!* well it *may* have been, but assuredly a *strange* fancy. I cannot comprehend that woman. She baffles my scrutiny. I have looked into her face with an eye she might well understand, were it indeed as I sometimes suspect, and she has been calm and unmoved. I have watched and studied her, still doubt—doubt—hideous doubt—is she what she seems, or—a TIGRESS?"

Mrs. Marston, on the other hand, procrastinated from day

to day the painful task of announcing to Mademoiselle de Barras the stern message with which she had been charged by her husband. And thus several weeks had passed, and she began to think that his silence upon the subject, notwithstanding his seeing the young French lady at breakfast every morning, amounted to a kind of tacit intimation that the sentence of banishment was not to be carried into immediate execution, but to be kept suspended over the unconscious offender.

It was now six or eight weeks since the hearse carrying away the remains of the ill-fated Sir Wynston Berkley, had driven down the dusky avenue; the autumn was deepening into winter, and as Marston gloomily trod the lonely woods of Dunoran, the withered leaves whirled drearily along his pathway, and the gusts that swayed the mighty branches above him were rude and ungenial. It was a bleak and sombre day, and as he broke into a long and picturesque vista, deep among the most sequestered woods, he suddenly saw before him, and scarcely twenty paces from the spot on which he stood, an apparition, which for some moments absolutely froze him to the earth.

Travel-soiled, tattered, pale, and wasted, John Merton, the murderer, stood before him. He did not exhibit the smallest disposition to turn about and make his escape. On the contrary, he remained perfectly motionless, looking upon his former master with a wild and sorrowful gaze. Marston twice or thrice essayed to speak; his face was white as death, and had he beheld the spectre of the murdered baronet himself, he could not have met the sight with a countenance of ghastlier horror.

"Take me, sir," said Merton, doggedly.

Still Marston did not stir.

"Arrest me, sir, in God's name—here I am," he repeated, dropping his arms by his side. "I'll go with you, wherever you tell me."

"Murderer!" cried Marston, with a sudden burst of furious horror—"murderer—assassin—miscreant!—take that."

And, as he spoke, he discharged one of the pistols he always carried about him full at the wretched man. The shot did not take effect, and Merton made no other gesture but to clasp his hands together, with an agonized pressure, while his head sunk upon his breast.

"Shoot me—shoot me," he said, hoarsely; "kill me like a dog: better for me to be dead than what I am."

The report of Marston's pistol had, however, reached another ear; and its ringing echoes had hardly ceased to vibrate among the trees, when a stern shout was heard not fifty yards away, and, breathless and amazed, Charles Marston sprang to the place. His father looked from Merton to him, and from him again to Merton, with a guilty and stupified scowl, still holding the smoking pistol in his hand.

"What—how! Good God—Merton!" ejaculated Charles.

"Ay, sir, Merton—ready to go to gaol, or wherever you will," said the man, recklessly.

"A murderer—a madman—don't believe him," muttered Marston, scarce audibly, with lips as white as wax.

"Do you surrender yourself, Merton?" demanded the young man, sternly, advancing toward him.

"Yes, sir; I desire nothing more—God knows I wish to die," responded he, despairingly, and advancing slowly to meet Charles.

"Come, then," said young Marston, seizing him by the collar—"come quietly to the house. Guilty and unhappy man, you are now my prisoner, and, depend upon it, I shall not let you go."

"I don't want to go, I tell you, sir. I have travelled fifteen miles to-day, to come here and give myself up to the master."

"Accursed madman!" said Marston, unconsciously gazing at the prisoner; and then suddenly rousing himself, he said, "Well, miscreant, you wish to die, and, by _____, you are in a fair way to *have* your wish."

"So best," said the man, doggedly. "I don't want to live— I wish I was in my grave—I wish I was dead a year ago."

Some fifteen minutes afterwards, Merton, accompanied by Marston and his son Charles, entered the hall of the mansion which, not ten weeks before, he had quitted under circumstances so guilty and terrible. When they reached the house, Merton seemed much agitated, and wept bitterly on seeing two or three of his former fellow-servants, who looked on him in silence as they passed, with a gloomy and fearful curiosity. These, too, were succeeded by others, peeping and whispering, and upon one pretence or another, crossing and re-crossing the hall, and stealing hurried glances at the criminal. Merton sate with his face buried in his hands, sobbing, and taking no note of the humiliating scrutiny of which he was the subject. Meanwhile, Marston, pale and agitated, made out his committal, and having sworn in several of his labourers and servants as special constables, dispatched the prisoner in their charge to the county gaol, where, under lock and key, we leave him in safe custody for the present.

After this event, Marston became excited and restless. He scarcely eat or slept, and his health seemed now as much shattered as his spirits had been before. One day he glided into the room in which, as we have said, it was Mrs. Marston's habit frequently to sit alone. His wife was there, and, as he entered, she uttered an exclamation of doubtful joy and surprise. He sate down near her in silence, and for some time looked gloomily on the ground. She did not care to question him, and anxiously waited until he should open the conversation. At length he raised his eyes, and, looking full at her, asked abruptly—

"Well, what about mademoiselle?"

Mrs. Marston was embarrassed, and hesitated.

"I told you what I wished with respect to that young lady some time ago, and commissioned you to acquaint her with my pleasure; and yet I find her still here, and apparently as much established as ever."

Again Mrs. Marston hesitated. She scarcely knew how to confess to him that she had not conveyed his message.

"Don't suppose, Gertrude, that I wish to find fault. I merely wanted to know whether you had told Mademoiselle de Barras, that we were agreed as to the necessity, or expediency, or what you please, of dispensing henceforward with her services. I perceive by your manner that you have not done so. I have no doubt your motive was a kind one, but my decision remains unaltered; and I now assure you again that I wish you to speak to her—I wish you explicitly to let her know my wishes and yours."

"Not *mine*, Richard," she answered, faintly.

"Well, *mine*, then," he replied, roughly. "We shan't quarrel about that."

"And when—how soon—do you wish me to speak to her on this, to both of us, most painful subject?" asked she, with a sigh.

"To-day—this hour—this minute, if you can; in short, the sooner the better," he replied, rising. "I see no reason for holding the thing back any longer. I am sorry my wishes were not complied with immediately. Pray, let there be no further hesitation or delay. I shall expect to learn this evening that all is arranged."

Marston having thus spoken, left her abruptly—went down to his study with a swift step—shut himself in, and throwing himself into a great chair, gave a loose to his agitation, which was extreme.

Meanwhile, Mrs. Marston had sent for Mademoiselle de Barras, anxious to get through her painful task as speedily as possible. The fair French girl speedily presented herself.

"Sit down, mademoiselle," said Mrs. Marston, taking her hand kindly, and drawing her to the prediëu chair beside herself.

Mademoiselle de Barras sate down, and, as she did so, read the countenance of her patroness with one rapid glance of her flashing eyes. These eyes, however, when Mrs. Marston looked at her the next moment, were sunk softly and sadly upon the floor. There was a heightened colour, however, in her cheek, and a quicker heaving of the bosom, which indicated the excitement of an anticipated and painful disclosure. The outward contrast of the two women, whose hands were so lovingly locked together, was almost as striking as the moral contrast of their hearts. The one, so chastened, sad, and gentle; the other, so capable of pride and passion— so darkly excitable, and yet, so mysteriously beautiful. The one, like a Niobe, seen in the softest moonshine; the other, a Venus, lighted in the glare of distant fires.

"Mademoiselle, dear mademoiselle, I am so much grieved at what I have to say, that I hardly know how to speak to you," said poor Mrs. Marston, pressing her hand; "but Mr. Marston has twice desired me to tell you, what you will hear with far less pain than it costs me to say it."

Mademoiselle de Barras stole another flashing glance at her companion, but did not speak.

"Mr. Marston still persists, mademoiselle, in desiring that we shall part."

"*Est-il-possible?*" cried the Frenchwoman, with a genuine start.

"Indeed, mademoiselle, you may well be surprised," said Mrs. Marston, encountering her full and dilated gaze, which, however, dropped again in a moment to the ground. "You may, indeed, naturally be surprised and shocked at this, to me, most severe decision."

"When did he speak last of it?" asked she, rapidly.

"But a few moments since," answered Mrs. Marston.

"Ha!" said mademoiselle, and remained silent and motionless for more than a minute.

"Madame," she cried at last, mournfully, "I suppose, then, I must go; but it tears my heart to leave you and dear Miss Rhoda. I would be very happy if, before departing, you would permit me, dear madame, once more to assure Mr. Marston of my innocence, and, in his presence, to call heaven to witness how unjust are all his suspicions."

"Do so, mademoiselle, and I will add my earnest assurances again; though, heaven knows," she said, despondingly, "I anticipate little success; but it is well to leave no chance untried."

Marston was sitting, as we have said, in his library. His agitation had given place to a listless gloom, and he leaned back in his chair, his head supported by his hand, and undisturbed except by the occasional fall of the embers upon the hearth. There was a knock at the chamber door. His back was toward it, and, without turning or moving, he called to the applicant to enter. The door opened—closed again—a light tread was audible—a tall shadow darkened the wall—Marston looked round, and Mademoiselle de Barras was standing before him. Without knowing how or why, he rose, and stood gazing upon her in silence.

"Mademoiselle de Barras," he said at last, in a tone of cold surprise.

"Yes, poor Mademoiselle de Barras," replied the sweet voice of the young Frenchwoman, while her lips hardly moved as the melancholy tones passed them.

"Well, Mademoiselle, what do you desire?" he asked, in the same cold accents, and averting his eyes.

"Ah, Monsieur, do you ask—can you pretend to be ignorant? Have you not sent me a message—a cruel, cruel message?"

She spoke so low and gently, that a person at the other end of the room could hardly have heard her words.

"Yes, Mademoiselle de Barras, I *did* send you a message," he replied, doggedly—"a cruel one you will scarcely presume to call it, when you reflect upon your own conduct, and the circumstances which have provoked the measures I have taken."

"What have I done, Monsieur?—what circumstances do you mean?" asked she, plaintively.

"What have you done! A pretty question truly—ha, ha!" he repeated, bitterly, and then added with suppressed vehemence—"ask your own heart, Mademoiselle."

"I have asked—I do ask, and my heart answers—*nothing*," she replied, raising her fine melancholy eyes for a moment to his face.

"It lies, then," he retorted, with a fierce scoff.

"Monsieur, before heaven I swear, you wrong me foully," she said earnestly, clasping her hands together.

"Did ever woman say she was accused *rightly*, Mademoiselle?" retorted Marston, with a sneer.

"I don't know—I don't care; I only know that *I* am innocent," continued she, piteously. "I call heaven to witness you have wronged me."

"Wronged you!—why, after all, with what have I charged you?" said he, scoffingly; "but let that pass. I have formed my opinions—arrived at my conclusions; if I have not named them broadly, you at least seem to understand their nature thoroughly. I know the world; I am no novice in the arts of women, Mademoiselle. Reserve your vows and attestations for schoolboys and simpletons; they are sadly thrown away upon me."

Marston paced to and fro, with his hands thrust into his pockets, as he thus spoke.

"Then you don't, or rather you will not believe what I tell you?" said she, imploringly.

"No," he answered, drily and slowly, as he passed her; "I don't, and I won't (as you say) believe one word of it, so, pray spare yourself any further trouble about the matter."

She raised her head, and darted after him a glance that seemed absolutely to blaze, and at the same time smote her little hand fast clenched upon her breast; the words, however, that trembled on her pale lips were not uttered; her eyes were again cast down, and her fingers played with the little locket that hung round her neck.

"I must make, before I go," she said, with a deep sigh and a melancholy voice, "one confidence—one last confidence; judge me by it. You cannot choose, but believe me now; it is a secret, and it must even here be *whispered, whispered, whispered!*"

As she spoke, the colour fled from her face, and her tones became so strange and resolute, that Marston turned short upon his heel and stopped before her. She looked in his face; he frowned, but lowered his eyes. She drew nearer, laid her hand upon his shoulder, and whispered for a few moments in his ear. He raised his face suddenly; its features were sharp and fixed; its hue was changed; it was livid and moveless, like a face cut in gray stone. He staggered back a little, and a little more, and then a little more, and fell backward. Fortunately the chair in which he had been sitting received him, and he lay there insensible as a corpse. When at last his eyes opened, there was no gleam of triumph—no shade of anger, nothing perceptible of guilt or menace in the young woman's countenance; the flush had returned to her cheeks; her dimpled chin had sunk upon her full, white throat; sorrow, shame, and pride seemed struggling in her handsome face; and she stood before him like a beautiful penitent, who has just made a strange and humbling shrift to her father confessor.

Next day, Marston was mounting his horse for a solitary ride through his park, when Doctor Danvers rode abruptly into the courtyard from the back entrance. Marston touched his hat, and said—

"I don't stand on forms with you, doctor, and you, I know, will waive ceremony with me. You will find Mrs. Marston at home."

"Nay, my dear sir," interrupted the clergyman, sitting firm in his saddle, "my business lies with *you* to-day."

"The devil it does!" said Marston, with discontented surprise.

"Truly it does, sir," repeated he, with a look of gentle reproof, for the profanity of Marston's ejaculation, far more than the rudeness of his manner, offended him, "and I grieve that your surprise should have somewhat carried you away——"

"Well, then, Doctor Danvers," interrupted Marston, drily, and without heeding his concluding remark, "if you really *have* business with me, it is, at all events, of no very pressing kind, and may be as well told after supper as now; so, pray, go into the house and rest yourself—we can talk together in the evening."

"My horse is not tired," said the clergyman, patting his steed's neck; "and if you do not object, I will ride by your side for a short time, and as we go, I can say out what I have to tell."

"Well, well, be it so," said Marston, with suppressed impatience, and without more ceremony, he rode slowly along the avenue, and turned off upon the soft sward in the direction of the wildest portion of his wooded demesne, the clergyman keeping close beside him. They proceeded some little way at a walk before Doctor Danvers spoke.

"I have been twice or thrice with that unhappy man," at length he said.

"*What* unhappy man?—unhappiness is no distinguishing singularity—is it?" said Marston, sharply.

"No, truly, you have well said," replied Dr. Danvers; "true it is that man is born unto trouble as the sparks fly upward. I speak, however, of your servant, Merton—a *most* unhappy wretch."

"Ha! you have been with *him*, you say?" replied Marston, with evident interest and anxiety.

"Yes, several times, and conversed with him long and gravely," continued the clergyman.

"Humph! I thought that had been the chaplain's business, not yours, my good friend," observed Marston.

"He has been unwell," replied Dr. Danvers; "and thus, for a day or two, I took his duty, and this poor man, Merton, having known something of me, preferred seeing me rather than a stranger—and so, at the chaplain's desire and his, I continued my visits."

"Well, and you have taught him to pray and sing psalms, I suppose; and what has come of it all?" demanded Marston, testily.

"He does pray, indeed—poor man! and I trust his prayers are heard with mercy at the throne of grace," said his companion, in his earnestness disregarding the scoffing tone of his companion. "He is full of compunction, and admits his guilt."

"Ho! that is well—well for *himself*—well for his *soul*, at least—you are sure of it—he confesses—confesses his guilt?"

Marston put his question so rapidly and excitedly, that the clergyman looked at him with a slight expression of surprise—and recovering himself, he added, in an unconcerned tone—

"Well, well—it was just as well he did so; the evidence is too clear for doubt or mystification; he knew he had no chance, and has taken the seemliest course—and, doubtless, the best for his hopes hereafter."

"I did not question him upon the subject," said Doctor Danvers; "I even declined to hear him speak upon it at first—but he told me he was resolved to offer no defence, and that he saw the finger of God in the fate which had overtaken him."

"He will plead guilty, then, I suppose?" suggested Marston, watching the countenance of his companion with an anxious and somewhat sinister eye.

"His words seem to imply so much," answered he; "and having thus frankly owned his guilt, and avowed his resolution to let the law take its due course in his case, without obstruction or evasion, I urged him to complete the grand work he had begun, and to confess to you, or to some other magistrate fully, and in detail, every circumstance connected with the perpetration of the dreadful deed."

Marston knit his brows, and rode on for some minutes in silence. At length, he said abruptly—

"In *this*, it seems to me, sir, you a little exceeded your commission."

"How so, my dear sir?" asked the clergyman.

"Why, sir," answered Marston, "the man may possibly change his mind before the day of trial, and it is the hangman's office, not yours, my good sir, to fasten the halter about his neck. You will pardon my freedom; but, were this deposition made as you suggest, it would undoubtedly hang him."

"God forbid, Mr. Marston," rejoined Danvers, "that I should induce the unhappy man to forfeit his last chances of escape, and to shut the door of human mercy against himself, but on this he seems already resolved; he says so; he has solemnly declared his resolution to me—and even against my warning, again and again reiterated the same declaration."

"That I should have thought quite enough, were I in your place, without inviting a detailed description of the whole process by which this detestable butchery was consummated. What more than the simple knowledge of the man's guilt does any mortal desire—guilty, or not guilty, is the plain question which the law asks, and no more; take my advice, sir, as a poor Protestant layman, and leave the arts of the confessional and inquisition to popish priests."

"Nay, Mr. Marston, you greatly misconceive me; as matters stand, there exists among the coroner's jury, and thus among the public, some faint and unfounded suspicion of the possibility of Merton's having had an accessory or accomplice in the perpetration of this foul murder."

"It is a lie, sir—a malignant, d_____d lie—the jury believe no such thing, nor the public neither," said Marston, starting in his saddle, and speaking in a voice of thunder; "you have been crammed with lies, sir; malicious, unmeaning, vindictive lies; lies invented to asperse my family, and torture my feelings—suggested in my presence by that scoundrel Mervyn, and scouted by the common sense of the jury."

"I do assure you," replied Doctor Danvers, in a voice

which seemed scarcely audible, after the stunning and passionate explosion of Marston's wrath, "I did not imagine that you could feel thus sorely upon the point; nay, I thought that you yourself were not without such painful doubts."

"Again, I tell you, sir," said Marston, in a tone somewhat calmer, but no less stern, "such doubts as you describe have *no* existence; your unsuspecting ear has been alarmed by a vindictive wretch, an old scoundrel who has scarce a passion left but spite towards me—few such there are, thank God— few such villains as would, from a man's very calamities, distil poison to kill the peace and character of his family."

"I am sorry, Mr. Marston," said the clergyman, "you have formed so ill an opinion of a neighbour, and I am very sure that Mr. Mervyn meant *you* no ill in frankly expressing whatever doubts still rested on his mind, after the evidence was taken."

"He did—the scoundrel!" said Marston, furiously striking his hand, in which his whip was clutched, upon his thigh— "he *did* mean to wound and torture me; and with the same object he persists in circulating what he calls his doubts. Meant me no ill! forsooth! why, my good God, sir, could any man be so stupid as not to perceive that the suggestion of such suspicions—absurd, contradictory, incredible as they were—was precisely the thing to exasperate feelings, God knows, sufficiently troubled already; and not content with raising the question, where it was scouted, as I said, as soon as named, the vindictive slanderer proceeds to propagate and publish his pretended surmises—d_____n him!"

"Mr. Marston, you will pardon me when I say that, as a Christian minister, I cannot suffer a spirit so ill as that you manifest, and language so unseemly as that you have just uttered, to pass unreproved," said Danvers, solemnly. "If you will cherish those bitter and unchristian feelings, at least for the brief space that I am with you, command your fierce, unbecoming words."

Marston was about to make a sneering retort, but restrained himself, and turned his head away.

"The wretched man himself appears now very anxious to make some further disclosures," resumed Doctor Danvers, after a pause, "and I recommended him to make them to *you*, Mr. Marston, as the most natural depository of such a statement."

"Well, Mr. Danvers, to cut the matter short, as it appears that a confession of some sort is to be made, be it so. I will attend and receive it. The judges will not be here for eight or ten weeks to come, so there is no great hurry about it. I shall ride down to the town, and see him in the jail some time within the next week."

With this assurance, Marston parted from the old clergyman, and rode on alone through the furze and fern of his wild and sombre park.

After supper that evening, Marston found himself alone in the parlour with his wife. Mrs. Marston availed herself of the opportunity to redeem her pledge to Mademoiselle de Barras. She was not aware of the strange interview which had taken place between him and the lady for whom she pleaded. The result of her renewed entreaties perhaps the reader has anticipated. Marston listened, doubted—listened, hesitated again—put questions, pondered the answers—debated the matter inwardly, and at last gruffly consented to give the young lady another trial, and permit her to remain for some time longer. Poor Mrs. Marston, little suspecting the dreadful truth, overwhelmed her husband with gratitude for granting to her entreaties (as he had predetermined to do) this fatal boon. Not caring to protract this scene—either from a disinclination to listen to expressions of affection, which had long lost their charm for him, and had become even positively distasteful, or perhaps from some instinctive recoil from the warm expression of gratitude from lips which, were the truth revealed, might justly have trembled with execration and reproach, he abruptly left the room, and Mrs. Marston, full of her good news, hastened, in the kindness of her heart, to communicate the fancied result of her advocacy to Mademoiselle de Barras.

It was about a week after this, that Marston was one evening surprised in his study by the receipt of the following letter from Dr. Danvers:—

"MY DEAR SIR,—You will be shocked to hear that Merton is most dangerously ill, and at this moment in imminent peril. He is thoroughly conscious of his situation, and himself regards it as a merciful interposition of Providence to spare him the disgrace and terror of the dreadful fate which he anticipated. The unhappy man has twice repeated his anxious desire, this day, to state some facts connected with the murder of the late Sir Wynston Berkley, which, he says, it is of the utmost moment that you should hear. He says that he could not leave the world in peace without having made this disclosure, which he especially desires to make to yourself, and entreats that you will come to receive his communication as early as you can in the morning. This is indeed needful, as the physician says that he is fast sinking. I offer no apology for adding my earnest solicitations to those of the dying man; and am, dear sir, your very obedient servant,

"J. DANVERS."

"He regards it as a merciful interposition of Providence!" muttered Marston, as he closed the letter, with a sneer. "Well, some men have odd notions of mercy and providence, to be sure; but if it pleases him, certainly I shall not complain, for one."

Marston was all this evening in better spirits than he had enjoyed for months, or even years. A mountain seemed to have been lifted from his heart. He joined in the conversation during and after supper, listened with apparent interest, talked with animation, and even laughed and jested. It is needless to say all this flowed not from the healthy cheer of a heart at ease, but from the excited and almost feverish sense of sudden relief.

Next morning, Marston rode into the old-fashioned assize town, at the further end of which the dingy and grated front of the jail looked warningly out upon the rustic passengers. He passed the sentries, and made his inquiries of the official at the hatch. He was relieved from the necessity of pushing these into detail, however, by the appearance of the physician, who at that moment passed from the interior of the prison.

"Doctor Danvers told me he expected to see you here this morning," said the medical man, after the customary salutation had been interchanged. "Your call, I believe, is connected with the prisoner John Merton."

"Yes, sir, so it is," said Marston. "Is he in a condition, pray, to make a statement of considerable length?"

"Far from it, Mr. Marston; he has but a few hours to live," answered the physician, "and is now insensible; but I believe he last night saw Doctor Danvers, and told him whatever was weighing upon his mind."

"Ha!—and can you say where Dr. Danvers now is?" inquired Marston, anxiously and hurriedly. "Not here, is he?"

"No; but I saw him, as I came here, not ten minutes since, ride into the town. It is market-day, and you will probably find him somewhere in the high street for an hour or two to come," answered he.

Marston thanked him, and, lost in abstraction, rode down to the little inn, entered a sitting-room, and wrote a hurried line to Dr. Danvers, entreating his attendance there, as a place where they might converse less interruptedly than in the street; and committing this note to the waiter, with the injunction to deliver it at once, and the information where Dr. Danvers was probably to be found, he awaited, with intense and agitating anxiety, the arrival of the clergyman.

It was not for nearly ten minutes, however, which his impatience magnified into an eternity, that the well-known voice of Dr. Danvers reached him from the little hall. It was in vain that Marston strove to curb his violent agitation: his heart swelled as if it would smother him; he felt, as it were, the chill of death pervade his frame, and he could scarcely see the door through which he momentarily expected the entrance of the clergyman.

A few minutes more, and Dr. Danvers entered the little apartment.

"My dear sir," said he, gravely and earnestly, as he grasped the cold hand of Marston, "I am rejoiced to see you. I have matters of great moment and the strangest mystery to lay before you."

"I dare say—I was sure—that is, I suspected so much," answered Marston, breathing fast, and looking very pale. "I heard at the prison that the murderer, Merton, was fast dying, and now is in an unconscious state; and from the physician, that you had seen him, at his urgent entreaty, last night. My mind misgives me, sir. I fear I know not what. I long, yet dread, to hear the wretched man's confession. For God's sake tell me, does it implicate anybody else in his guilt?"

"No; no one specifically; but it has thrown a hideous

additional mystery over the occurrence. Listen to me, my dear sir, and the whole narrative, as he stated it to me, shall be related now to you," said Dr. Danvers.

Marston had closed the door carefully, and they sate down together at the further end of the apartment. Marston, breathless and ghastly pale; his lips compressed—his brows knit—and his dark, dilated gaze fixed immovably upon the speaker. Dr. Danvers, on the other hand, tranquil and solemn, and with, perhaps, some shade of awe overcasting the habitual sweetness of his countenance.

"His confession was a strange one," renewed Dr. Danvers, shaking his head gravely. "He said that the first idea of the crime was suggested by Sir Wynston's man accidentally mentioning, a few days after their arrival, that his master slept with his bank-notes, to the amount of some hundreds of pounds, in a pocket-book under his pillow. He declared that as the man mentioned this circumstance, something muttered the infernal suggestion in his ear, and from that moment he was the slave of that one idea; it was ever present with him. He contended against it in vain—he dreaded and abhorred it; but still it possessed him; he felt his power of resistance yielding. This horrible stranger which had stolen into his heart, waxed in power and importunity, and tormented him day and night. He resolved to fly from the house. He gave notice to you and Mrs. Marston of his intended departure; but accident protracted his stay until that fatal night which sealed his doom. The influence which had mastered him, forced him to rise from his bed, and take the knife—the discovery of which afterwards helped to convict him—and led him to Sir Wynston's chamber; he entered—it was a moonlight night."

Here the clergyman, glancing round the room, lowered his voice, and advanced his lips so near to Marston that their heads nearly touched. In this tone and attitude he continued his narrative for a few minutes. At the end of this brief space, Marston rose up slowly, and with a movement backward, every feature strung with horror, and saying, in a long whisper, the one word, "yes," which seemed like the hiss of a snake before he makes his last deadly spring. Both were silent for a time. At last Marston broke out with hoarse vehemence—

"Dreadful—horrible—oh, God! God!—my God! how frightful!"

And throwing himself into a chair, he clasped his hands across his eyes and forehead, while the sweat of agony literally poured down his pale face.

"Truly it is so," said the clergyman, scarcely above his breath; and, after a long interval—"horrible, indeed!"

"Well," said Marston, rising suddenly to his feet, wiping the dews of horror from his face, and looking wildly round, like one newly waked from a nightmare, "I must make the most of this momentous and startling disclosure. I shall spare no pains to come at the truth," said he, energetically. "Meanwhile, my dear sir, for the sake of justice and of mercy, observe secrecy. Leave me to sift this matter; give no note anywhere that we *suspect*. Observe this reserve and security, and with it, detection will follow. Breathe but one word, and you arm the guilty with double caution, and turn licentious gossip loose upon the fame of an innocent and troubled family. Once more I entreat—I expect—I implore silence— silence, at least, for the present—*silence!*"

"I quite agree with you, my dear Mr. Marston," answered Dr. Danvers. "I have not divulged one syllable of that poor wretch's confession, save to yourself alone. You, as a magistrate, a relative of the murdered gentleman, and the head of that establishment among whom the guilt rests, are invested with an interest in detecting, and powers of sifting the truth in this matter, such as none other possesses. I clearly see with you, too, the inexpediency and folly of talking, for talking's sake, of this affair. I mean to keep my counsel, and shall most assuredly, irrespectively even of your request—which should, however, of course, have weight with me—maintain a strict and cautious silence upon this subject."

Some little time longer they remained together, and Marston, buried in strange thoughts, took his leave, and rode slowly back to Dunoran.

Months passed away—a year, and more—and though no new character appeared upon the stage, the relations which had subsisted among the old ones became, in some respects, very materially altered. A gradual and disagreeable change came over Mademoiselle de Barras's manner; her affectionate attentions to Mrs. Marston became less and less frequent; nor was the change merely confined to this growing coldness; there was something of a positive and still more unpleasant kind in the alteration which we have noted. There was a certain independence and *insouciance*, conveyed in a hundred intangible but significant little incidents and looks—a something which, without being open to formal rebuke or remonstrance, yet bordered, in effect, upon impertinence, and even insolence. This indescribable and provoking self-assertion, implied in glances, tones, emphasis, and general bearing, surprised Mrs. Marston far more than it irritated her. As often as she experienced one of these studied slights or insinuated impertinences, she revolved in her own mind all the incidents of their past intercourse, in the vain endeavour to recollect some one among them which could possibly account for the offensive change so manifest in the conduct of the young Frenchwoman.

Mrs. Marston, although she sometimes rebuked these

artful affronts by a grave look, a cold tone, or a distant manner, yet had too much dignity to engage in a petty warfare of annoyance, and had, in reality, no substantial and well-defined ground of complaint against her, such as would have warranted her either in taking the young lady herself to task, or in bringing her conduct under the censure of Marston.

One evening it happened that Mrs. Marston and Mademoiselle de Barras had been left alone together after the supper-party had dispersed. They had been for a long time silent, and Mrs. Marston resolved to improve the *tête-à-tête*, for the purpose of eliciting from mademoiselle an explanation of her strange behaviour.

"Mademoiselle," said she, "I have lately observed a very marked change in your conduct to me."

"*Indeed!*" said the Frenchwoman.

"Yes, mademoiselle; you must be yourself perfectly aware of that change; it is a studied and intentional alteration," continued Mrs. Marston, in a gentle but dignified tone; "and although I have felt some doubt as to whether it were advisable, so long as you observe toward me the forms of external respect, and punctually discharge the duties you have undertaken, to open any discussion whatever upon the subject; yet I have thought it better to give you a fair opportunity of explaining frankly, should you desire to do so, the feelings and impressions under which you are acting."

"Ah, you are very obliging, madame," said she, coolly.

"It is quite clear, mademoiselle, that you have either misunderstood me, or that you are dissatisfied with your situation among us: your conduct cannot otherwise be accounted for," said Mrs. Marston, gravely.

"My conduct—*ma foi!* what conduct?" retorted the handsome Frenchwoman, confidently, and with a disdainful glance.

"If you question the fact, mademoiselle," said the elder lady, "it is enough. Your ungracious manner and ungentle looks, I presume, arise from some apparently sufficient and well-defined cause, of which, however, I know nothing."

"I really was not aware," said Mademoiselle de Barras, with a supercilious smile, "that my looks and my manner were subjected to so rigid a criticism, or that it was my duty to regulate both according to so nice and difficult a standard."

"Well, mademoiselle," continued Mrs. Marston, "it is plain that whatever may be the cause of your dissatisfaction, you are resolved against confiding it to me. I only wish to know frankly from your own lips, whether you have formed a wish to leave this situation: if so, I entreat of you to declare it freely."

"You are very obliging, indeed, madame," said the pretty foreigner, drily, "but I have no such wish, at least at present."

"Very well, mademoiselle," replied Mrs. Marston, with gentle dignity; "I regret your want of candour, on your own account. You would, I am sure, be much happier, were you to deal frankly with me."

"May I now have your permission, madame, to retire to my room?" asked the French girl, rising, and making a low courtesy—"that is, if madame has nothing further to censure."

"Certainly, mademoiselle; I have nothing further to say," replied the elder lady.

The Frenchwoman made another and a deeper courtesy, and withdrew. Mrs. Marston, however, heard, as she was designed to do, the young lady tittering and whispering to herself, as she lighted her candle in the hall. This scene mortified and grieved poor Mrs. Marston inexpressibly. She was little, if at all, accessible to emotions of anger, and certainly none such mingled in the feelings with which she regarded Mademoiselle de Barras. But she had found in this girl a companion, and even a confidante in her melancholy solitude; she had believed her affectionate, sympathetic, tender, and the disappointment was as bitter as unimagined.

The annoyances which she was fated to receive from Mademoiselle de Barras, were destined, however, to grow in number and in magnitude. The Frenchwoman sometimes took a fancy, for some unrevealed purpose, to talk a good deal to Mrs. Marston, and on such occasions would persist, notwithstanding that lady's marked reserve and discourage-ment, in chatting away, as if she were conscious that her conversation was the most welcome entertainment possible to her really unwilling auditor. No one of their interviews did she ever suffer to close without in some way or other suggesting or insinuating something mysterious and untold to the prejudice of Mr. Marston. Those vague and intangible hints, whose meaning, for an instant legible and terrific, seemed in another moment to dissolve and disappear, tortured Mrs. Marston like the intrusions of some spectre, vanishing as soon as revealed; and this, along with the portentous change, rather *felt* than visible, in mademoiselle's conduct toward her, invested the beautiful Frenchwoman, in the eyes of her former friend and patroness, with an indefinable character that was not only repulsive but formidable.

Mrs. Marston's feelings with respect to this person were still further disturbed by the half-conveyed hints and innuendoes of her own maid, who never lost an opportunity of insinuating her intense dislike of the Frenchwoman, and appeared perpetually to be upon the very verge of making some explicit charges, or some shocking revelations, respecting her, which, however, she as invariably evaded; and even when Mrs. Marston once or twice insisted upon her explaining her meaning distinctly, she eluded her mistress's desire, and left her still in the same uneasy uncertainty.

Marston, on his part, however much his conduct might tend to confirm suspicion, certainly did nothing to dissipate the painful and undefined apprehensions respecting himself, which Mademoiselle de Barras, with such malign and mysterious industry, laboured to raise. His spirits and temper were liable to strange fluctuations. In the midst of that excited gaiety, to which, until lately, he had been so long a stranger, would sometimes intervene paroxysms of the blackest despair, all the ghastlier for the contrast, and with a suddenness so abrupt and overwhelming, that one might have fancied him crossed by the shadow of some terrific apparition, unseen by all but his own fascinated gaze. Sometimes, for a whole day, or even more, he would withdraw himself from the society of his family, and, in morose and moody solitude, take his meals alone in his library, and steal out unattended to wander among the thickets and glades of his park. Sometimes, again, he would sit for hours in the room which had been Sir Wynston's, and, with a kind of horrible resolution, often loiter there till after nightfall. In such hours, the servants would listen with curious awe, as they heard his step, pacing to and fro, in that deserted and inauspicious chamber, while his voice, in broken sentences, was also imperfectly audible, as if maintaining a muttered dialogue. These eccentric practices gradually invested him, in the eyes of his domestics, with a certain preternatural mystery, which enhanced the fear with which they habitually regarded him, and was subsequently confirmed by his giving orders to have the furniture taken out of the ominous suite of rooms, and the doors nailed up and secured. He gave no reason for this odd and abrupt measure, and gossip of course reported that the direction had originated in his having encountered the spectre of the murdered baronet, in one of these strange and unseasonable visits to the scene of the fearful catastrophe.

In addition to all this, Marston's conduct towards his wife became strangely capricious. He avoided her society more than ever, and when he did happen to exchange a few words with her, they were sometimes harsh and violent, and, at others, remorsefully gentle and sad, and this without any changes of conduct upon her part to warrant the wayward uncertainty of his treatment. Under all these circumstances, Mrs. Marston's unhappiness and uneasiness greatly increased. Mademoiselle de Barras, too, upon several late occasions, had begun to assume a tone of authority and dictation which justly offended the mistress of the establishment. Meanwhile Charles Marston had returned to Cambridge, and Rhoda, no longer enjoying those happy walks with her brother, which had been made still more happy by their often leading her into the society of her young neighbours of Newton Park, pursued her light and easy studies with Mademoiselle de Barras, and devoted her leisure hours to the loved society of her mother.

One day Mrs. Marston, sitting in her own room with Rhoda, had happened to call in her own maid, to take down and carefully dust some richly-bound volumes which filled a bookcase in the little chamber.

"You have been crying, Willett," said Mrs. Marston, observing that the young woman's eyes were red and swollen.

"Indeed and I was, ma'am," she replied, reluctantly, "and I could not help it, so I could not."

"Why, what has happened to vex you—has any one ill-treated you?" said Mrs. Marston, who had an esteem for the poor girl. "Come—come—you must not fret about it; only tell me what has vexed you. Come, come, you really must not be foolish."

"Oh! ma'am, no one has ill-used *me*, ma'am; but I can't but be vexed sometimes, ma'am, and fretted to see how things is going on. I have one wish—just one wish, ma'am— and if I got *that*, I'd ask no more," said the girl.

"And what *is* it?" asked Mrs. Marston; "what do you wish for?—speak plainly, Willett, what is it?"

"Ah! ma'am, if I said it maybe you might not be pleased. Don't ask me, ma'am," said the girl, dusting the books very hard, and tossing them down again with angry emphasis. "I don't desire anybody's harm, God knows, but for all that I wish what I wish, and that is the truth."

"Why, Willett, I really cannot account for your strange habit of lately hinting, and insinuating, and always speaking riddles, and refusing to explain your meaning. What *do* you mean?—speak plainly; if there are any dishonest practices going on, it is your duty to say so distinctly."

"Oh! ma'am, it is just a wish I have. I wish——; but it's no matter. If I could once see the house clear of that Frenchwoman——"

"If you mean Mademoiselle de Barras, she is a *lady*," interrupted Mrs. Marston.

"Well, ma'am, I beg pardon," continued the woman; "lady or no lady, it is all one to me; for I am very sure, ma'am, she'll never leave the house till there is something bad comes about; and—and——. I can't bring myself to talk to you about her, ma'am. I can't say what I want to tell you; but— but——. Oh, ma'am, for God's sake, try and get her out, any way, no matter how—try and get rid of her."

As she said this, the poor girl burst into a passionate

agony of tears, and Mrs. Marston and Rhoda looked on in silent amazement, while she for some minutes continued to sob and weep.

The party were suddenly recalled from their various reveries by a knock at the chamber-door—it opened, and the subject of the girl's deprecatory entreaty entered. There was something unusually excited and assured in Mademoiselle de Barras's air and countenance; perhaps she had a suspicion that she had been the topic of their conversation. At all events, she looked round upon them with a smile, in which there was something supercilious, and even defiant; and, without waiting to be invited, sate herself down with a haughty air.

"I was about to ask you to sit down, mademoiselle, but you have anticipated me," said Mrs. Marston, gravely. "You have something to say to me, I suppose; I am quite at leisure, so pray let me hear it now."

"Thank you—thank you, madame," replied she, with a sharp, and even scornful glance; "I ought to have asked your permission to sit; I forgot to do so; but you have condescended to give it without my doing so; that was very kind—very kind, indeed."

"But I wish to know, mademoiselle, whether you have anything very particular to say to me?" said Mrs. Marston.

"You wish to know!—and why, pray, madame?" asked Mademoiselle de Barras, sharply.

"Because, unless it is something very urgent, I should prefer your talking to me some other time; as, at present, I desire to be alone with my daughter."

"Oh, ho! I ought to ask pardon again," said mademoiselle, with the same glance, and the same smile. "I find I am *de trop*—quite in the way. *Helas!* I am very unfort-unate to-day."

Mademoiselle de Barras made not the slightest

movement, and it was evident that she was resolved to prolong her stay, in sheer defiance of Mrs. Marston's wishes.

"Mademoiselle, I conclude from your silence that you have nothing very pressing to say, and therefore must request that you will have the goodness to leave me for the present," said Mrs. Marston, who felt that the spirit of the French girl's conduct was too apparent not to have been understood by Rhoda and the servant, and that it was of a kind, for example sake, impossible to be submitted to, or tolerated.

Mademoiselle de Barras darted a fiery and insolent glance at Mrs. Marston, and was, doubtless, upon the point of precipitating the open quarrel which was impending, by setting her authority at defiance; but she checked herself, and changed her line of operations.

"We are not alone, madame," she said, with a heightened colour, and a slight toss of the head. "I was about to speak of Mr. Marston. I had something—not much, I confess—to say; but before servants I shan't speak—nor, indeed, now at all. So, madame, as you desire it, I shall not further interrupt you. Come, Miss Rhoda, come to the music-room, if you please, and finish your practice for to-day."

"You forget, mademoiselle, that I wish to have my daughter with me at present," said Mrs. Marston.

"I am very sorry, madame," said the French lady, with the same heightened colour and unpleasant smile, and her finely-pencilled brows just discernibly knit, so as to give a novel and menacing expression to her beautiful face—"I am very sorry, madame, but she must, so long as I remain accountable for her education, complete her allotted exercises at the appointed hours; and nothing shall, I assure you, with my consent, interfere with these duties. Come, Miss Rhoda, precede me, if you please, to the music-room. Come, come."

"Stay where you are, Rhoda," said Mrs. Marston, firmly

and gently, and betraying no symptom of excitement, except in a slight tremor of her voice, and a faint flush upon her cheek.—"Stay where you are, my dear child. I am your *mother*, and, next to your father, have the first claim upon your obedience. Mademoiselle," she continued, addressing the Frenchwoman, calmly but firmly, "my daughter will remain here for some time longer, and you will have the goodness to withdraw. I insist upon it, Mademoiselle de Barras."

"I will not leave the room, I assure you, madame, without my pupil," retorted mademoiselle, with resolute insolence. "Your husband, madame, has invested me with this authority over my pupil, and she *shall* obey me. Miss Rhoda, I say again, go down to the music-room."

"Remain where you are, Rhoda," said Mrs. Marston again. "Mademoiselle, you have long been acting as if your object were to provoke me to part with you. I find it impossible any longer to overlook this grossly disrespectful conduct—conduct of which I had, indeed, believed you absolutely incapable. Willett," she continued, addressing the maid, who was evidently bursting with rage at the scene she had just witnessed—"your master is, I believe, in the library—go down, and tell him that I entreat him to come here immediately."

The maid started on her mission with angry alacrity, darting a venomous glance at the handsome Frenchwoman as she passed.

Mademoiselle de Barras, meanwhile, sate, listless and defiant, in her chair, and tapping her little foot with angry excitement upon the floor. Rhoda sate close by her mother, holding her hand fast, and looking frightened, perplexed, and as if she were on the point of weeping. Mrs. Marston, though flushed and excited, yet maintained her dignified and grave demeanour. And thus, in silence, did they all three await the arrival of the arbiter to whom Mrs. Marston had so promptly appealed.

A few minutes more, and Marston entered the room. Mademoiselle's expression changed as he did so to one of dejected and sorrowful submission; and, as Marston's eye lighted upon her, his brow darkened, and his face grew pale.

"Well, well—what is it?—what is all this?" he said, glancing with a troubled eye from one to the other. "Speak, some one. Mrs. Marston, *you* sent for me—what is it?"

"I want to know, Mr. Marston, from your own lips," said the lady, in reply, "whether Rhoda is to obey me or Mademoiselle de Barras?"

"Bah!—a question of women's prerogative," said Marston, with muttered vehemence.

"Of a *wife's* and a *mother's* prerogative, Richard," said Mrs. Marston, with gentle emphasis; "a very simple question, and one I should have thought needing no deliberation to decide it."

"Well, child," said he, turning to Rhoda, with angry irony, "pray what is all this fuss about? You are a very ill-used young lady, I dare aver. Pray what cruelties does Mademoiselle de Barras propose inflicting upon you, that you need to appeal thus to your mother for protection?"

"You quite mistake me, Richard," interposed Mrs. Marston; "Rhoda is perfectly passive in this matter. I simply wish to learn from you, in mademoiselle's presence, whether I or she is to command my daughter?"

"*Command!*" said Marston, evading the direct appeal; "and pray what is all this *commanding* about?—what do you want the girl to do?"

"I wish her to remain here with me for a little time, and mademoiselle, knowing this, desires her instantly to go to the music-room, and leave me. That is all," said Mrs. Marston.

"And pray, is there nothing to make her going to the music-room advisable or necessary? Has she no music to learn, or studies to pursue? Psha! Mrs. Marston, what needs all this noise about nothing? Go, miss," he added, sharply and peremptorily, addressing Rhoda—"go this moment to the music-room."

The girl glided from the room, and mademoiselle, as she followed, shot a glance at Mrs. Marston, which wounded and humbled her in the dust.

"Oh! Richard, Richard, if you knew all, you would not have subjected me to this indignity," she said; and throwing her arms about his neck, she wept, for the first time for many a long year, upon his breast.

Marston was embarrassed and agitated. He disengaged her arms from his neck, and placed her gently in a chair. She sobbed on for some time in silence—a silence which Marston himself did not essay to break. He walked to the door, apparently with the intention of leaving her. He hesitated, however, and returned; took a hurried turn through the room; hesitated again; sat down; then returned to the door, not to depart, but to close it carefully, and walked gloomily to the window, whence he looked forth, buried in agitating and absorbing thoughts.

"Richard, to you this seems a trifling thing; but indeed it is not so," said Mrs. Marston, sadly.

"You are very right, Gertrude," he said, quickly, and almost with a start; "it is very far from a trifling thing; it is very important."

"You don't blame me, Richard?" said she.

"I blame nobody," said he.

"Indeed, I never meant to offend you, Richard," she urged.

"Of course not; no, no; I never said so," he interrupted, sarcastically; "what could you gain by that?"

"Oh! Richard, better feelings have governed me," she said, in a melancholy and reproachful tone.

"Well, well, I suppose so," he said; and after an interval, he added, abstractedly, "This cannot, however, go on; no, no—it *cannot*. Sooner or later, it must have come; better at once—better *now*."

"What do you mean, Richard?" she said, greatly alarmed, she knew not why. "What are you resolving upon? Dear Richard, in mercy tell me. I implore of you, tell me."

"Why, Gertrude, you seem to me to fancy that, because I don't talk about what is passing, that I don't *see* it either. Now this is quite a mistake," said Marston, calmly and resolutely. "I have long observed your growing dislike of Mademoiselle de Barras. I have thought it over; this *fracas* of to-day has determined me—it is decisive. I suppose you now wish her to *go*, as earnestly as you once wished her to stay. You need not answer. I know it. I neither ask nor care to whose fault I am to attribute these changed feelings—female caprice accounts sufficiently for it; but whatever the cause, the effect is undeniable; and the only way to deal satisfactorily with it, is to dismiss mademoiselle peremptorily and at once. You need take no part in the matter; I take it all upon myself. To-morrow morning she shall have left this house. I have said it, and am perfectly resolved."

As he thus spoke, as if to avoid the possibility of any further discussion, he turned abruptly from her, and left the room.

The extreme agitation which she had just undergone, combined with her physical delicacy to bring on an hysterical attack; and poor Mrs. Marston, with an aching head and a heavy heart, lay down upon her bed. She had swallowed an opiate, and before ten o'clock upon that night, an eventful one as it proved, she had sunk into a profound slumber.

Some hours after this, she became in a confused way conscious of her husband's presence in the room. He was walking, with an agitated mien, up and down the chamber, and casting from time to time looks of great trouble toward the bed where she lay. Though the presence of her husband was a strange and long unwonted occurrence there, and at such an hour, and though she felt the strangeness of the visit, the power of the opiate overwhelmed her so, that she could only see this apparition gliding back and forward before her with the passive wonder and curiosity with which one awaits the issue of an interesting dream.

For a time she lay once more in an uneasy sleep; but still, throughout even this, she was conscious of his presence; and when, a little while after, she again saw him, he was not walking to and fro before the foot of the bed, but sitting beside her, with one hand laid upon the pillow on which her head was resting, the other supporting his chin. He was looking steadfastly upon her, with a changed face, an expression of bitter sorrow, compunction, and tenderness. There was not one trace of sternness; all was softened. The look was what she fancied he might have turned upon her had she lain there dead, ere yet the love of their early and ill-fated union had grown cold in his heart. There was something in it which reminded her of days and feelings, gone never to return. And while she looked in his face with a sweet and mournful fascination, tears unconsciously wet the pillow on which her poor head was resting. Unable to speak, unable to move, she heard him say—

"It was not your fault, Gertrude—it was not yours, nor mine. There is a destiny in these things too strong for us. Past is past—what is done, is done for ever; and even were it all to do over again, what power have I to mend it! No, no; how could I contend against the combined power of passions, circumstances, influences—in a word, of FATE? You have been good and patient, while I——but no matter. Your lot, Gertrude, is a happier one than mine."

Mrs. Marston heard him and saw him, but she had not the power, nor even the will, herself to speak or move. He appeared before her passive sense like the phantasm of a dream. He stood up at the bedside, and looked on her steadfastly, with the same melancholy expression. For a moment he stooped over her, as if about to kiss her face, but checked himself, stood erect again at the bedside, then suddenly turned—the curtain fell back into its place, and she saw him no more.

With a strange mixture of sweet and bitter feelings, this vision rested upon the memory of Mrs. Marston, until, gradually, deep slumber again overcame her senses, and the incident and all its attendant circumstances faded into oblivion.

It was past eight o'clock when Mrs. Marston awoke next morning. The sun was shining richly and cheerily in at the windows; and as the remembrance of Marston's visit to her chamber, and the unwonted manifestations of tenderness and compunction which accompanied it, returned, she felt something like hope and happiness, to which she had long been a stranger, flutter her heart. The pleasing reverie, to which she was yielding, was, however, interrupted. The sound of stifled sobbing in the room reached her ear, and, pushing back the bed-curtains, and leaning forward to look, she saw her maid, Willett, sitting with her back to the wall, crying bitterly, and striving, as it seemed, to stifle her sobs with her apron, which was wrapped about her face.

"Willett—Willett, is it *you* who are sobbing? What is the matter with you, child?" said Mrs. Marston, anxiously.

The girl checked herself, dried her eyes hastily, and walking briskly to a little distance, as if engaged in arranging the chamber, she said, with an affectation of carelessness— "Oh, ma'am, it is nothing—nothing at all, indeed, ma'am."

Mrs. Marston remained silent for a time, while all her vague and agonizing apprehensions returned. Meantime the girl continued to shove the chairs hither and thither, and to arrange and disarrange everything in the room, with a fidgety industry, intended to cover her agitation. A few minutes, however, served to weary her of this; for she abruptly stopped, stood by the bedside, and, looking at her mistress, burst into tears.

"Good God! what is it?" said Mrs. Marston, shocked and even terrified, while new alarms displaced the old ones. "Is Miss Rhoda—can it be—is she—is my darling well?"

"Oh yes, ma'am," answered the maid—"very well, ma'am; she is up, and out walking, and knows nothing of all this."

"All *what?*" urged Mrs. Marston. "Tell me—tell me, Willett, what has happened. What is it? Speak, child—say what it is."

"Oh, ma'am—oh, my poor, dear mistress!" continued the girl, and stopped, almost stifled with sobs.

"Willett, you must speak—you must say what is the matter. I implore of you—I desire you!" urged the distracted lady. Still the girl, having made one or two ineffectual efforts to speak, continued to sob.

"Willett, you will drive me mad. For mercy's sake—for God's sake, speak—tell me what it is!" cried the unhappy lady.

"Oh, ma'am, it is—it is about the master," sobbed the girl.

"Why he can't—he has not—Oh, merciful God! he has not hurt himself!" she almost screamed.

"No, ma'am—no—not *himself*—no—no—but——" and again she hesitated.

"But what? Speak out, Willett—dear Willett, have mercy on me, and speak out," cried her wretched mistress.

"Oh, ma'am, don't be fretted—don't take it to heart, ma'am," said the maid, clasping her hands together in anguish.

"Anything—anything, Willett—only speak at once," she answered.

"Well, ma'am, it is soon said—it is easy told. The master, ma'am—the master is gone with the Frenchwoman; they went in the travelling coach last night, ma'am—he is gone away with her, ma'am—that is all."

Mrs. Marston looked at the girl with a gaze of stupified, stony terror—not a muscle of her face moved—not one heaving respiration showed that she was living. Motionless, with this fearful look fixed upon the girl, and her thin hands stretched towards her, she remained, second after second; at last her outstretched hands began to tremble more and more violently—and as if, for the first time the knowledge of his calamity had reached her—with a cry, unearthly, as though body and soul were parting, she fell back motionless in her bed.

Several hours had passed before Mrs. Marston was restored to consciousness; to this state of utter insensibility, one of silent, terrified stupor succeeded—and it was not until she saw her daughter Rhoda standing at her bedside, weeping, that she found voice and recollection to speak.

"My child—my darling—my poor child," she cried, sobbing piteously, as she drew her to her heart, and looked in her face alternately—"my darling—my darling child."

Rhoda could only weep, and return her poor mother's caresses in silence. Too young and inexperienced to understand the full extent and nature of this direful calamity— the strange occurrence—the general and apparent consternation of the whole household, and the spectacle of her mother's agony, had filled her with fear, perplexity, and anguish. Scared and stunned with a vague sense of danger, like a young bird, that, for the first time, cowers under a thunder-storm, she nestled in her mother's bosom—there, with a sense of protection, and with a feeling of boundless love and tenderness, she lay, frightened, wondering, and weeping.

Two or three days passed, and Dr. Danvers came and sate for several hours with poor Mrs. Marston. To comfort and console, were, of course, out of his power. The nature of the bereavement—far more terrible than death—its recent occurrence—the distracting consciousness of all its complicated consequences—rendered this a hopeless task. She bowed herself under the blow, with the submission of a broken heart. The hope to which she had clung for years had vanished—the worst that ever her imagination feared, had come in earnest.

One idea was now constantly present in her mind. She felt a sad, but immovable assurance, that she should not live long, and the thought—"What will become of my darling, when I am gone—who will guard and love my child when I am in my grave—whom is she to look to for tenderness and protection then?" perpetually haunted her, and superadded the pangs of a still wilder despair to the desolation of a broken heart.

It was not for more than a week after this event, that, one day, Willett, with a certain air of anxious mystery, entered the silent and darkened chamber where Mrs. Marston lay—she had a letter in her hand—the seal and handwriting were Mr. Marston's. It was long before the injured wife was able to open it—when she did so, the following sentences met her eye:—

"GERTRUDE—You can be ignorant neither of the nature, nor of the consequences of the decisive step I have taken—I do not seek to excuse it. For the censure of the world—its meddling and mouthing hypocrisy—I care absolutely nothing. I have long set it at defiance—and you yourself, Gertrude, when you deliberately reconsider the circumstances of estrangement and coldness under which, though beneath the same roof, we have lived for years—without either sympathy or confidence, can scarcely—if at all—regret the rupture of a tie which had long ceased to be anything better than an irksome and galling formality—I do not desire to attribute to you the smallest blame. There was an incompatibility, not of temper, but of feelings, which made us *strangers*, though calling one another man and wife—upon this fact I rest my own justification; our living together under these circumstances was, I dare say, equally undesired by us both. It was, in fact, but a deference to the formal hypocrisy of the world. At all events, the irrevocable act which separates us for ever is done—and I have now merely to state so much of my intentions as may relate in anywise to your future arrangements. I have written to your cousin, and former guardian, Mr. Roe, telling him how matters stand between us. You, I told him, shall have, without opposition from me, the whole of your own fortune to your own separate use, together with whatever shall be mutually agreed upon as reasonable, from my income, for your support, and that of my daughter. It will be necessary to complete your arrangements with expedition, as I purpose returning to Dunoran in about three weeks—and as, of course, a meeting between you and those by whom I shall be accompanied is wholly out of the question, you will see the expediency of losing no time in adjusting everything for your's, and my daughter's departure. In the details, of course, I shall not interfere. I think I have made myself clearly intelligible, and would recommend your communicating at once with Mr. Roe, with a view to completing temporary arrangements, until your final plans shall have been decided upon.

"RICHARD MARSTON."

The reader can easily conceive the feelings with which this letter was perused. We shall not attempt to describe them; nor shall we weary his patience by a detail of all the circumstances attending Mrs. Marston's departure. Suffice it to mention, that, in less than a fortnight after the receipt of the letter which we have just copied, she had for ever left the mansion of Dunoran.

In a small house, in a sequestered part of the beautiful county of Wicklow, the residence of Mrs. Marston and her daughter was for the present fixed. And there, for a time, the heartbroken and desolate lady enjoyed, at least, the privilege of an immunity from the intrusions of all external troubles. But the blow, under which the feeble remains of her health and strength were gradually to sink, had struck too surely home—and, from month to month—almost from week to week—the progress of decay was perceptible.

Meanwhile, though grieved and humbled, and longing to return to Ireland, to comfort his unhappy mother, Charles Marston, for the present absolutely dependant upon his father, had no choice but to remain at Cambridge, and to pursue his studies there.

At Dunoran, Marston and the partner of his guilt continued to live. The old servants were all gradually dismissed, and new ones hired by Mademoiselle de Barras. There they dwelt, shunned by everybody, in a stricter and more desolate seclusion than ever. The novelty of the unrestraint and licence of their new mode of life speedily passed away, and with it the excited and guilty sense of relief, which had for a time produced a false and hollow gaiety. The sense of security prompted in mademoiselle a hundred indulgences, which, in her former precarious position, she would not have dreamed of. Outbreaks of temper, sharp, and sometimes violent, began to manifest themselves on her part—and renewed disappointment, and blacker remorse, to darken the mind of Marston himself. Often, in the dead of night, the servants would overhear their bitter and fierce altercations ringing through the melancholy mansion—and often the reckless use of terrible and mysterious epithets of crime. Their quarrels increased in violence and in frequency—and, before two years had passed, feelings of bitterness, hatred, and dread, alone seemed to subsist between them. Yet, upon Marston she continued to exercise a powerful and mysterious influence. There was a dogged, apathetic submission upon his part, and a growing insolence upon her's, constantly more and more strikingly visible. Neglect, disorder, and decay, too, were more than ever apparent in the dreary air of the place.

Part III

D R. DANVERS, save by rumour and conjecture, knew nothing of Marston and his abandoned companion. He had, more than once, felt a strong disposition to visit Dunoran, and expostulate, face to face, with its guilty proprietors. This idea, however, he had, upon consideration, dismissed; not on account of any shrinking from the possible repulses and affronts to which the attempt might subject him—but from a thorough conviction that the endeavour would be utterly fruitless for good, while it might, very obviously, expose him to painful misinterpretation and suspicion—leaving it to be imagined that he had been influenced, if by no meaner motive, at least by the promptings of an idle and prying curiosity, in thus pushing his way within the proscribed precincts of Dunoran.

Meanwhile, he maintained a correspondence with Mrs. Marston, and had even once or twice since her departure visited her, when business had called him to the capital, at her new place of abode. Latterly, however, this correspondence had been a good deal interrupted, and its intervals had been supplied occasionally by Rhoda; whose letters, although she herself appeared unconscious of the mournful event whose approach they too plainly indicated, were painful records of the manifest and rapid progress of mortal decay.

He had just received one of those ominous letters, at the little post-office in the town we have already mentioned, and full of the melancholy news it contained, Dr. Danvers was riding slowly towards his home. As he rode into a lonely road, traversing a hilly tract of some three miles in length, the singularity, it may be, of his costume attracted the eye of another passenger, who was, as it turned out, no other than Marston himself. For two or three miles of this desolate road, their ways happened to lie together. Marston's first impulse was to avoid the clergyman; his second—which he obeyed—was to join company, and ride along with him, at all events, for so long as would show that he shrank from no encounter which fortune or accident presented. There was a spirit of bitter defiance in this, which cost him a painful effort.

"How do you do, Parson Danvers?" said Marston, touching his hat with the handle of his whip.

Danvers thought he had seldom seen a man so changed in so short a time. His face had grown sullen and wasted, and his figure slightly stooped, with an appearance of feebleness.

"Mr. Marston," said the clergyman, gravely, and with some embarrassment, "it is a long time since you and I have seen one another, and many and painful events have passed in the interval. I scarce know upon what terms we meet. I am prompted to speak to you, and in a tone, perhaps, which you will hardly brook; and yet, if we keep company, as it seems likely we may, I cannot, and I ought not, to be silent."

"Well, Mr. Danvers, I accept the condition—speak what you will," said Marston, gloomily. "If you exceed your privilege, and grow uncivil, I need but use my spurs, and leave you behind me preaching to the winds."

"Ah! Mr. Marston," said Doctor Danvers, almost sadly, after a considerable pause; "when I saw you close beside me, my heart was troubled within me."

"You looked on me as something from the nether world, and expected to see the cloven hoof," said Marston, bitterly, and raising his booted foot a little as he spoke; "but, after all, I am but a vulgar sinner of flesh and blood, without enough of the preternatural about me to frighten an old nurse, much less to agitate a pillar of the church."

"Mr. Marston, you talk sarcastically; but you *feel* that recent circumstances, as well as old recollections, might well disturb and trouble me at sight of you," answered Dr. Danvers.

"Well—yes—perhaps it is so," said Marston, hastily and sullenly, and became silent for a while.

"My heart is full, Mr. Marston—charged with grief, when I think of the sad history of those with whom, in my mind, you must ever be associated," said Dr. Danvers.

"Ay, to be sure," said Marston, with stern impatience; "but, then, you have much to console you. You have got your comforts and your respectability—all the dearer, too, from the contrast of other people's misfortunes and degradations; then you have your religion, moreover——"

"Yes," interrupted Danvers, earnestly, and hastening to avoid a sneer upon this subject; "God be blessed, I am an humble follower of his gracious Son, our Redeemer; and though, I trust, I should bear with patient submission whatever chastisement in his wisdom and goodness he might see fit to inflict upon me, yet I do praise and bless him for the mercy which has hitherto spared me, and I do feel that mercy all the more profoundly, from the afflictions and troubles with which I daily see others overtaken."

"And in the matter of piety and decorum, doubtless, you bless God also," said Marston, sarcastically, "that you are not as other men are, nor even as this publican."

"Nay, Mr. Marston; God forbid I should harden my sinful heart with the wicked pride of the Pharisee. Evil and corrupt am I already—over much. Too well I know the vileness of my heart, to make myself righteous in my own eyes," replied Dr. Danvers, humbly. "But, sinner as I am, I am yet a messenger of God, whose mission is one of authority to his fellow-sinners; and woe is me if I speak not the truth at all seasons, and in all places, where my words may be profitably heard."

"Well, Doctor Danvers, it seems you think it your duty to speak to me, of course, respecting my conduct and my spiritual state. I shall save you the pain and trouble of opening the subject—I shall state the case for you in two words," said Marston, almost fiercely. "I have put away my wife without just cause, and am living in sin with another woman. Come, what have you to say on this theme? Speak out. Deal with me as roughly as you will, I will hear it, and answer you again."

"Alas, Mr. Marston! and do not these things trouble you?" exclaimed Dr. Danvers, earnestly. "Do they not weigh heavy upon your conscience? Ah, sir, do you not remember that, slowly and surely, you are drawing towards the hour of death, and the day of judgment?"

"The hour of death! Yes, I know it is coming, and I await it with indifference. But, for the day of judgment, with its books and trumpets! my dear doctor, pray don't expect to frighten me with that."

Marston spoke with an angry scorn, which had the effect of interrupting the conversation for some moments.

"Am I to understand, Mr. Marston," asked Dr. Danvers, after a considerable pause, "that you reject revealed religion wholly, or that you confine your scepticism to one point?"

"I reject it wholly," replied Marston, coldly.

"Do you believe even in God the Creator?" urged Dr. Danvers, with a mixture of earnest simplicity and horror.

"Ay, in a creator I do believe," answered he, "but not in the creator you have painted. I do not say in my heart there is no God; but I say, and believe, there is no such God as you describe and worship. The thing is a mass of contradictions. Take but the first, and most hacknied of the set. You tell me he is infinitely powerful. Well, suppose I assent to that, what do you tell me next? Why, that he is infinitely benevolent, too! Well, what should be the necessary practical result of both these attributes? Why, of course, that his creatures should be happy to the extent of their capabilities of happiness. And how does this inference square with the common facts of experience? Psha, my dear sir, even in these, your fundamental postulates, appear the weakness and confusion of falsehood."

"You have made the difficulty yourself. You misinterpret terms, and force upon the doctrines of the Bible a meaning they were never intended to bear," answered Doctor Danvers. "God's will asserts itself progressively—by intermediate agencies—by a graduated system of cause and effect; but, in the end, and as respects the purpose to which it tends, irresistibly, omnipotently. Thus, in one sense——"

"Tut, tut, my good sir, the word 'omnipotence' has but one meaning. But, enough of this," interrupted Marston; "you cannot give me new convictions, or shake my old ones. I thank you, nevertheless, for taking so much trouble, though in vain. In truth, doctor, you find me, in spiritual matters, but a sorry and singularly unpromising subject—what *you* will term an inveterate and dogged infidel, but, as I believe, an unprejudiced man, of plain, common sense, and with a most unaccommodating contempt for cant and mummery of every sort. I have my creed—such as it is. It has served me thus far, and for the brief term I have yet to live, it will do very well."

"Yet, pardon me if I pursue this a moment longer. You acknowledge a benevolent Creator," persisted Dr. Danvers, who, even at the risk of offending his companion, endeavoured to prolong the discussion.

"No, *not* a benevolent one," interrupted Marston, fiercely; "a malignant, or, at best, a reckless one, if you will. Why, look around you; see disease—madness—hunger—hatred. Psha, sir! seeing all these, how dare you insult common sense by calling the creator of them infinitely—that is the word—*infinitely* benevolent. If *you* carried with you everywhere, by day and night, a load of accumulated, and all but unendurable misery, produced by the natural working of the very elements which your Creator himself combined in your character, and of the circumstances among which he, with his own hand, plunged you—if you were such a wretch as I am—you would cease to prate of his mercy and his justice. Psha, sir; I despise this snivel, and laugh at your creed, as scornfully as he himself does."

"Mr. Marston, your language shocks as well as grieves me," said Dr. Danvers; "you speak as though you *hated* the light, with a railing and a bitter spirit. May God, in his mercy, soften and illuminate your heart—may He, by the wonderful working whereby He subdueth all things unto himself, even yet subdue your stubborn unbelief, and pour his grace into your heart, that so, at last, your precious soul may be delivered out of the sorrows and anguish which, even now, overwhelm it like a stormy sea."

They rode on, side by side, for a long time, without speaking. At length, however, Marston unexpectedly broke the silence—

"Doctor Danvers," said he, "you asked me some time ago if I feared the hour of death, and the day of judgment. I answered you truly, I do *not* fear them—nay *death*, I think, I could meet with a happier and a quieter heart than any other chance that can befall me; but there are other fears—fears that *do* trouble me much."

Doctor Danvers looked inquiringly at him; but neither spoke for a time.

"You have not seen the catastrophe of the tragedy yet," said

Marston, with a stern, stony look, made more horrible by a forced smile, something like a shudder. "I wish I could tell you—*you*, Doctor Danvers—for you are honourable and gentle-hearted. I wish I durst tell you what I fear—the only, *only* thing I really do fear. Oh, God—oh, God! No mortal knows it but myself, and I see it coming upon me with slow, but unconquerable might. Oh, God—dreadful spirit—spare me!"

Again they were silent, and again Marston resumed—

"Doctor Danvers, don't mistake me," he said, turning sharply, and fixing his eyes with a strange expression upon his companion. "I dread nothing *human*—I fear neither death, nor disgrace, nor eternity; I have no secrets to keep—no exposures to apprehend; but I dread—I dread——"

He paused—scowled darkly, as if stung with pain—turned away, muttering to himself—and gradually became much excited and agitated.

"I can't tell you now, sir, and I won't," he said, abruptly and fiercely, and with a countenance darkened with a wild and appalling rage that was wholly unaccountable. "I see you searching me with your eyes. Suspect what you will, sir, you shan't inveigle me into admissions. Ay, pry—whisper—stare—question, conjecture, sir—I suppose I must endure the world's impertinence, but, d_____n me if I gratify it."

They rode on slowly for fully ten minutes in utter silence, except that Marston occasionally muttered to himself, as it seemed, in excited abstraction. Danvers had at first felt naturally offended at the violent and insulting tone in which he had been so unexpectedly and unprovokedly addressed; but this feeling of irritation was but transient, and some fearful suspicions as to Marston's sanity flitted through his mind. In a calmer and more dogged tone, his companion now addressed him—

"There is little profit, you see, doctor, in worrying me

about your religion," said Marston. "It is but sowing the wind, and reaping the whirlwind; and, to say the truth, the longer you pursue it the less I am in the mood to listen. If ever *you* are cursed and persecuted as I have been, you will understand how little tolerant of gratuitous vexations and contradictions a man may become. We have squabbled over religion long enough, and each holds his own faith still. Continue to sun yourself in your happy delusions, and leave me untroubled to tread the way of my own dark and cheerless destiny."

Thus saying, he made a sullen gesture of farewell, and spurring his horse, crossed the broken fence at the roadside, and so, at a listless pace, through gaps and by farm-roads, penetrated towards his melancholy and guilty home.

It was shortly after this, that a new arrival at Dunoran excited the curiosity of the neighbourhood. A rather good-looking, but over-dressed Frenchman, with a free-and-easy assurance which might have passed him off as the master of the place, of a sudden made his appearance. This foreigner styled himself the Count de Barras, and was rumoured to be the brother of "mademoiselle." With the exception, however, of his tall and somewhat tawdry exterior, and of the very slender information we have just summed up, nothing whatever was known about him; and as he seldom, if ever, stirred beyond the precincts of the demesne, it was conjectured that his necessities, rather than any pleasanter influence, had brought him there; those, moreover, whose opportunities for conjecture were pronounced to be the most favourable, reported that he possessed, on his arrival, no visible endowments beyond a huge appetite and a single change of clothes. Such as he was, however, he became domesticated at Dunoran; and it is scarcely necessary to add, that this new importation was little calculated to add to the respectability and character of the establishment.

Two years had now passed since the decisive event which had for ever separated Marston from her who had loved him so devotedly and so fatally—two years to him of disappointment, abasement, and secret rage; two years to her of gentle and heart-broken submission to the chastening hand of heaven. At the end of this time she died. Marston read the letter that announced the event with a stern look, and silently, but the shock he felt was terrific. No man is so self-abandoned to despair and degradation, that at some casual moment thoughts of amendment—some gleams of hope, however faint and transient, from the distant future—will not visit him. With Marston, those thoughts had somehow ever been associated with vague ideas of a reconciliation with the being whom he had forsaken—good and pure, and looking at her from the darkness and distance of his own fallen state, almost angelic as she seemed. But she was now dead—he could make her no atonement—she could never smile forgiveness upon him. This long-familiar image—the last that had reflected for him one ray of the lost peace and love of happier times, had vanished, and henceforward there was before him nothing but storm, and darkness, and fear.

Consequent upon this event, however, were certain new arrangements, involving in their issue important results to several of the persons of this tale. Marston's embarrassed fortunes made it to him an object to resume the portion of his income heretofore devoted to the separate maintenance of his wife and daughter. In order to effect this, it became, of course, necessary to recall his daughter Rhoda, and fix her residence once more at Dunoran. No more dreadful penalty could have been inflicted upon the poor girl—no more agonising ordeal than that she was thus doomed to undergo. She had idolised her mother, and now adored her memory. She knew that Mademoiselle de Barras had betrayed and indirectly murdered the parent she had so devotedly loved; she knew that that woman had been the curse, the fate of her family, and she regarded her naturally with feelings of mingled terror and abhorrence, the intensity of which was indescribable. To find herself, then, forced to reside with this fearful and revolting woman, to keep her company, to submit perhaps to her government, and daily to witness her usurpation of the place and prerogative of the dear and gentle parent who was gone—could imagination have conceived a more intolerable and heart-rending penance!

The few scattered friends and relatives, whose sympathies had been moved by the melancholy fate of poor Mrs. Marston, and who cared to inquire about the arrangements made for her maintenance, were unanimously agreed that the intended removal of the young and innocent daughter to the polluted mansion of sin and shame, was too intolerably revolting to be permitted. But each of these virtuous individuals unhappily thought it the duty of the others to interpose, and felt himself no individual obligation to offer this pure and lovely child of misfortune an asylum from the snares and horrors of the evil scene to which she was now summoned as her home. Everybody's business, as the adage hath it, was in this case nobody's; and with a running commentary of wonder and reprobation, and much virtuous criticism, events were suffered uninterruptedly to take their sinister and melancholy course.

It was about two months after the death of Mrs. Marston, and on a bleak and ominous night at the wintry end of autumn, that poor Rhoda, in deep mourning, and pale with grief and agitation, descended from a chaise at the well-known door of the mansion of Dunoran. Whether from consideration for her feelings, or, as was more probable, from pure indifference, Rhoda was conducted on her arrival direct to her own chamber, and it was not until the next morning that she saw her father. He entered her room unexpectedly; he was very pale, and as she thought, greatly altered, but he seemed perfectly collected and free from agitation. The marked and even shocking change in his appearance, and perhaps even the trifling though painful circumstance that he wore no mourning for the beloved being who was gone, caused her, after a moment's mute gazing in his face, to burst into an irrepressible flood of tears.

Marston waited stoically until the paroxysm had subsided, and then taking her hand, with a look in which a dogged sternness was contending with something like shame, he said—

"There, there; you can weep when I am gone. I shan't say very much to you at present, Rhoda, and only wish you to attend to me for one minute. Listen, Rhoda—the lady whom you have been in the habit (here he slightly averted his eyes) of calling Mademoiselle de Barras, is no longer so; she is married; she is my wife, and consequently you will treat her with the respect due to"—he would have said, "a mother," but could not, and supplied the phrase by adding, "to that relation."

Rhoda was unable to speak, but almost unconsciously bowed her head in token of attention and submission, and her father pressed her hand more kindly, as he continued—

"I have always found you a dutiful and obedient child, Rhoda, and expected no other conduct from you. Mrs. Marston will treat you with proper kindness and consideration, and desires me to say that you can, whenever you please, keep strictly to yourself, and need not, unless you feel so disposed, attend the regular meals of the family. This privilege may suit your present depressed spirits, especially as Monsieur de Barras, Mrs. Marston's brother, is a stranger to you, and you are aware, of course, that he is our guest at present."

She had not known this before, but the intelligence, strange to say, was not unwelcome, inasmuch as any thing or person likely to interfere between her and the dreaded society of her former governess, was to her an unspeakable relief.

After a few words more, Marston withdrew, leaving his daughter to her reflections, and bleak and bitter enough they were.

Some weeks passed away, and perhaps we shall best consult our reader's ease by substituting for the formal precision of narrative, a few extracts from the letters which Rhoda wrote to her brother, still at Cambridge. These will convey her own impressions respecting the scenes and personages among whom she was now to move.

"The house and place are much neglected, and the former in some parts suffered almost to go to decay. The windows broken in the last storm, nearly eight months ago, they tell me, are still unmended, and the roof, too, unrepaired. The pretty garden near the well, among the lime-trees, that our darling mother was so fond of, is all but obliterated with weeds and grass, and since my first visit I have not had heart to go near it again. All the old tenants are gone—new faces everywhere. . . . .

"I have been obliged several times, through fear of offending my father, to join the party in the drawing-room. You may conceive what I felt at seeing mademoiselle in the place once filled by our dear mamma. I was so choked with sorrow, bitterness, and indignation, and my heart so palpitated, that I could not speak, and I believe they thought I was going to faint. Mademoiselle looked very angry, but my father pretending to show me, heaven knows what, from the window, led me to it, and the air revived me a little. Mademoiselle (for I cannot call her by her new name) is altered a good deal—more, however, in the character than the contour of her face and figure. Certainly, however, she has grown a good deal fuller, and her colour is higher; and whether it is fancy or not, I cannot say, but certainly to me it seems that the expression of her face has acquired something habitually lowering and malicious, and which, I know not how, inspires me with an undefinable dread. She has, however, been tolerably civil to me, but seems contemptuous and rude to my father, and I am afraid he is very wretched. I have seen them exchange such looks, and overheard such intemperate and even appalling altercations between them, as indicate something worse and deeper than ordinary ill-will. This makes me additionally wretched, especially as I cannot help thinking that some mysterious cause enables her to frighten and tyrannise over my poor father. I sometimes think he absolutely detests her; yet, though fiery altercations ensue, he ultimately submits to this bad and cruel woman. Oh, my dear Charles, you have no idea of the shocking, or rather the terrifying reproaches I have heard interchanged between them, as I accidentally passed the room where they were sitting—such terms as have sent me to my room, feeling as if I were in a horrid dream, and make me cry and tremble for hours after I got there. . . . . I see my father very seldom, and when I do, he takes but little notice of me. . . . . Poor Willett, you know, returned with me. She accompanies me in my walks, and is constantly dropping hints about mademoiselle, from which I know not what to gather. . . .

. . . . Monsieur de Barras, mademoiselle's brother, is, in my opinion, a particularly offensive person—vulgar, loud, and almost insultingly familiar. Willett says he has not a penny of money but what he extracts from mademoiselle, and that he has come here to live upon my father, which, indeed, is not unlikely. The first day I saw him, he made a point of staring and ogling in so marked and offensive a way, that I felt at once angry and ashamed, and the more I marked my displeasure and annoyance, the more familiar he became, as if resolved, by some abominable perversity, to construe my very dislike into a species of encouragement. Another day I met him in the hall alone, and he instantly began to grin, and sigh, and jabber love speeches. I did not so much as look back at him, but walked straight on in silence, and trying to appear as unconcerned as if he had not been there. But this kind of rebuke seems thrown away upon him, for he recommenced the same practices no later than yesterday; and when I was leaving the room, with an insufferable affectation of playfulness he ran before me, and stood between me and the door. I was really both incensed and frightened. Whereupon mademoiselle, who just entered at the other door, in a towering passion, attacked him with furious volubility; and, to do him justice, he looked thoroughly cowed. I think, however, she has greatly mistaken my part in the matter, for she has looked very angrily on me ever since. But that is, I need scarcely tell you, to me a matter of very complete indifference. . . . .

"I often fear that my father has some secret and mortal ailment. He generally looks ill, and sometimes quite *wretchedly*. He came twice lately to my room, I think to speak to me on some matter of importance; but he said only a sentence or two, and even these broken and incoherent. He seemed unable to command spirits for the interview; and, indeed, he grew so agitated and strange, that I was alarmed, and felt greatly relieved when he left me. . . . .

"I do not, you see, disguise my feelings, dear Charles. I do not conceal from you the melancholy and anguish of my present situation. How intensely I long for your promised arrival. I have not a creature to whom I can say one word in confidence, except poor Willett; who, though very good-natured, and really dear to me, is yet far from being a companion. I sometimes think my intense anxiety to see you here is almost selfish; for I know you will feel as acutely as I do the terrible change observable everywhere. But I cannot help longing for your return, dear Charles, and counting the days and the very hours till you arrive. . . . .

"Be cautious, in writing to me, not to say anything which you would not wish mademoiselle to see; for Willett tells me that she *knows* that she often examines, and even intercepts the letters that arrive; and, though Willett may be mistaken, and I hope she is, yet it is better that you should be upon your guard. Ever since I heard this, I have brought my letters to the post-office myself, instead of leaving them with the rest upon the hall table; and you know it is a long walk for me. . . . .

"I go to church every Sunday, and take Willett along with me. No one from this seems to think of doing so but ourselves. I see the Mervyns there. Mrs. Mervyn is particularly kind, and Emily grown quite beautiful. The good old lady constantly regrets the 'invincible prejudice,' as she calls it, which would prevent, of course, my father's permitting me to visit them. I know that what she wishes is to offer me an asylum at Newton Park; and you cannot think with how much tenderness and delicacy she conveys the wish. But I dare not hint the subject to my father; and, earnestly as I desire it, I could not but feel that I should go there, not to visit, but to *reside.* And so, even in this, in many respects, delightful project, is mingled the bitter apprehension of dependence—something so humiliating, that, kindly and delicately as the offer is made, I could not bring myself to embrace it. I have a great deal to say to you, and long to see you.". . . . .

These extracts will enable the reader to form a tolerably accurate idea of the general state of affairs at Dunoran. Some particulars must, however, be added. In writing to her brother, Rhoda greatly understated the real unhappiness and apprehensions involved in her present situation. The impertinent attentions of Monsieur de Barras were not only to her a source of disgust and indignation, but of no small anxiety and alarm. The utter seclusion of the house, buried far among gloomy masses of timber—the desolate extent, and comparative desertion of the mansion itself—her own isolated and defenceless position, friendless and companionless—and, more than all, her consciousness of the degradation and baseness of the characters by whom she was surrounded—all these circumstances filled her mind with melancholy and alarms, vague, indeed, but incessant, and often almost intolerable.

Marston, meanwhile, continued to be the same gloomy and joyless being as heretofore. Sometimes moody and apathetic—sometimes wayward, and even savage—but never for a moment at ease—never social; an isolated, disdainful, ruined man.

One day as Rhoda sate and read under the shade of some closely inwoven evergreens, in a lonely and sheltered part of the neglected pleasure-grounds, with her honest maid, Willett, in attendance, she was surprised by the sudden appearance of her father, who stood unexpectedly before her. Though his attitude for some time was fixed, his countenance was troubled with a restless anxiety and pain, and his sunken eyes rested upon her with a fiery and fretted gaze. He seemed lost in agitated thought for a while, and then, touching Willett sharply on the shoulder, said abruptly—

"Go. I shall call you when you are wanted. Walk down that alley;" and, as he spoke, he indicated with his walking-cane the course he desired her to take.

When the maid was sufficiently distant to be quite out of hearing, Marston sate down beside Rhoda upon the bench, and took her hand in silence. His grasp was cold, and alternately relaxed and contracted with an agitated uncertainty, while his eyes were fixed upon the ground, and he seemed meditating how to open the conversation. At last, as if suddenly awaking from a fearful reverie, he said—

"You correspond with Charles?"

"Yes, sir," she replied, with the respectful formality prescribed by the usages of the time, "we correspond regularly."

"Ay, ay—and, pray, when did you last hear from him?" he continued.

"About a month since, sir," she replied.

"Ha!—and—and—was there nothing strange— nothing—nothing mystic and menacing in his letter? Come, come, you know what I speak of"—he stopped abruptly, and stared in her face with an agitated gaze.

"No, indeed, sir; there was not anything of the kind," she replied.

"I have been greatly shocked—I may say incensed," said Marston, excitedly, "by a passage in his last letter to me. Not that it says anything specific; but—but it amazes me; it enrages me."

He again checked himself, and Rhoda, much surprised, and even shocked, said, stammeringly—"I am sure, sir, that dear Charles would not intentionally say or do anything that could offend you."

"Ah! as to that, I believe so, too. But it is not with *him* I am indignant—no, no. Poor Charles, I believe, he *is*, as you say, disposed to conduct himself as a son ought to do—respectfully and obediently. Yes, yes—Charles is very well; but I fear he is leading a bad life, notwithstanding—a very bad life: he is becoming subject to *influences* which never visit or torment the good—believe me he is."

Marston shook his head, and muttered to himself, with a look of almost craven anxiety, and then whispered to his daughter—

"Just read this, and then tell me is it not so. Read it—read it—and pronounce."

As he thus spoke, he placed in her hand the letter of which he had spoken, and with the passage to which he invited her attention folded down. It was to the following effect:—

> "I cannot tell you how shocked I have been by a piece of information conveyed to me in an anonymous letter, and which is of so very delicate a nature that without your special command I should hesitate to pain you by its recital. I trust it may be utterly false; it nevertheless suggests inquiry. It is enough to say that it is of a very horrible nature, and affects the lady (Mademoiselle de Barras) whom you have recently honoured with your hand."

"Now you see," cried Marston, with a shuddering fierceness, as she returned the letter with a blanched cheek and trembling hand—"now you see it all. Are you stupid?—the stamp of the cloven hoof—eh?"

Rhoda, unable to gather his meaning, but, at the same time, with a heart full and trembling, stammered a few frightened words, and became silent.

"It is *he*, I tell you, that does it all; and if Charles were not living an evil life, he could not have spread his nets for him," said Marston, vehemently. "He can't go near anything good; but, like a scoundrel, he knows where to find a congenial nature, and when he does, he has skill enough to practise upon it. I know him well, and his arts and his smiles—ay, and his scowls and his grins, too. He goes, like his master, up and down, and to and fro upon the earth, for ceaseless mischief. There is not a friend of mine he can get hold of, but he whispers in his ear some damned slander of me. He is drawing them all into a common understanding against me; and he takes an actual pleasure in telling me how the thing goes on—how, one after the other, he has converted my friends into conspirators and libellers, to blast my character, and take my life, and now the monster essays to lure my children into the hellish confederation."

"Who is he, father—who is he?" faltered Rhoda.

"You never saw him," retorted Marston, sternly. "No, no; you can't have seen him, and you probably never will; but if he *does* come here again, don't listen to him—he is half-fiend and half-idiot, and no good comes of his mouthing and muttering. Avoid him, I warn you—avoid him. Let me see—how shall I describe him?—let me see. You remember—you remember Berkley, Sir Wynston Berkley—well, he greatly resembles that dead villain; he has all the same grins, and shrugs, and monkey airs, and his face and figure are like. But *he* is a grimed, ragged, wasted piece of sin, little better than a beggar—a shrunken, malignant libel on the human shape. Avoid him, I tell you—avoid him; he is steeped in lies and poison, like the very serpent that betrayed us. Beware of him, I say; for if he once gains your ear, he will delude you, spite of all your vigilance; he will make you his accomplice—and thenceforth inevitably there is nothing but mortal and implacable hatred between us!"

Frightened at this wild language, Rhoda did not answer, but looked up in his face in silence. A fearful transformation was there—a scowl so livid and maniacal, that her very senses seemed leaving her with terror. Perhaps the sudden alteration observable in her countenance, as this spectacle of hideous menace so unexpectedly encountered her, recalled him to himself; for he added hurriedly, and in a tone of gentler meaning—

"Rhoda, Rhoda, watch and pray. My daughter, my child! keep your heart pure, and nothing bad can approach you for ill. No, no; you are good, and the good need not fear!"

Suddenly Marston burst into tears, as he ended this sentence, and wept long and convulsively. She did not dare to speak, or even to move; but after a while he ceased, appeared uneasy, half ashamed and half angry; and looking with a horrified and bewildered glance into her face, he said—

"Rhoda, child, what—what have I said? My God! what have I been saying? Did I—do I look ill? Oh, Rhoda, Rhoda, may you never feel this!"

He turned away from her without awaiting her answer, and walked away with the appearance of intense agitation, as if to leave her. He turned again, however, and with a face pallid and sunken as death, approached her slowly—

"Rhoda," said he, "don't tell what I have said to any one—don't, I conjure you, even to Charles. I speak too much at random, and say more than I mean—a foolish, rambling habit—so do not repeat one word of it—not one word to any living mortal. You and I, Rhoda, must have our little secrets."

He ended with an attempt at a smile, so obviously painful and fear-stricken, that as he walked hurriedly away, the astounded girl burst into a bitter flood of tears. What was—

what could be the meaning of the shocking scene she had then been forced to witness? She dared not answer the question. Yet one ghastly doubt haunted her like her shadow—a terrific suspicion, that the malign and hideous light of madness was already glaring upon his mind. As leaning upon the arm of her astonished attendant, she retraced her steps, the trees, the flowers, the familiar hall-door, the echoing passages—every object that met her eye, seemed strange and unsubstantial, and she gliding on among them in a horrid dream.

Time passed on: there was no renewal of the painful scene which dwelt so sensibly in the affrighted imagination of Rhoda. Marston's manner was changed towards her; he seemed shy, cowed, and uneasy in her presence, and thenceforth she saw less than ever of him. Meanwhile the time approached which was to witness the long-expected, and, by Rhoda, the intensely prayed for arrival of her brother.

Some four or five days before this event, Mr. Marston having, as he said, some business in Dublin, and further designing to meet his son there, took his departure from Dunoran, leaving poor Rhoda to the guardianship of her guilty stepmother, and the persecutions of the coarse and insolent Frenchman, who, with a free-and-easy audacity, had established himself as one of the family; and although she had seen so little of her father, yet the very consciousness of his presence had given her a certain confidence, and sense of security, which vanished at the moment of his departure. Fear-stricken and wretched as he had been, his removal, nevertheless, seemed to her to render the lonely and inauspicious mansion still more desolate and ominous than before.

This vague feeling of apprehension and melancholy

foreshadowed the painful realities which were to follow. Strangely enough, the departure of Mr. Marston was apparently as much felt, though in a different way, by Monsieur de Barras, as by the unhappy and unsophisticated girl, who so justly disliked and feared him. His loathed attentions became more and more pushing and audacious, and at the same time, from some mysterious reason, the new mistress of the house regarded her with a countenance more threatening and malignant than heretofore. She had, with a vague and instinctive antipathy, avoided all contact and intercourse with Mrs. Marston, or as, for distinctness sake, we shall continue to call her, "Mademoiselle," since her return; and she on her part had appeared to acquiesce with a sort of scornful nonchalance, in the tacit understanding that she and her former pupil should see and hear as little as might be of one another. With these angry and suspicious glances, however, to which we have alluded, there supervened a galling disposition to throw out sarcastic hints, and bitter, though mysterious insinuations, which insulted and alarmed the innocent girl, and deepened and confirmed the intense abhorrence with which she had habitually shrunk from all intercourse with her.

Meanwhile poor Willett, with her good-natured honesty and her inexhaustible gossip, endeavoured to amuse and re-assure her young mistress, and sometimes even with some partial success. One day, as she assisted her to dress, her prattle accidentally turned upon a subject of some little interest.

"That mounseer is a queer sort of a man, miss—a queer sort of a *gentleman*, so he is. Don't you think so yourself, miss?" asked the maid.

"I have not had many opportunities of judging, Willett: but I confess that I have not seen much to admire in him," answered the young lady, who freely admitted the confidential privilege assumed by her attached attendant.

"I tell you what it is, Miss Rhoda, there is something I don't like going on between him and 'Madam the governess.' I think the two of them is hatching some mischief," pursued the maid; "they are always grumbling and muttering at one another, as if both was finding fault, and both blaming the other; and the minute any one goes into the room, they pretend to be talking quite quiet and natural; and then they will be hugger-muggering and whispering together quite friendly after it all, for an hour and more; and then they look so queer if I happen to come in of a sudden; and when they walk out together, you'll see them talking and talking away as fast, and never a smile on their faces, but looking round them now and then, like as if they were afraid some one might be listening to them, and then walking on another bit, and stopping with the eagerness of talking to one another, and standing stock-still for five minutes together."

"Well, and what of all that, Willett?" inquired Rhoda.

"What!—why it looks very like plotting, that is all, miss; plotting, I say, and—and——; but no matter, I can't talk of that yet; but I think I'll find out something before long about them, that will open the eyes of some people—that is all; but no matter, all in good time," replied Willett.

Rhoda looked inquisitively at her, and the maid, in pity to the curiosity she had excited, added, after a time, in a somewhat frightened whisper—

"I am nearly sure of one thing, miss, between them they have made a pretty fool of the master. Wait a while, miss, and I will be able to tell you more. There will be terrible work about it yet, and that you'll find, miss; but I cannot tell you more for a while."

Rhoda found little, it may be imagined, in these and

similar hints and surmises, to calm the uneasy sensations awakened by her own lonely and defenceless position. She avoided, of course, as far as it was possible, any likelihood of meeting the impudent foreigner; and justly as she abhorred the society of her former governess, it was nevertheless with no small satisfaction that she remarked, as it seemed, a studious anxiety on her part, to prevent his ever succeeding in procuring a *tête-à-tête* with her.

Their combined management, however, failed occasionally of its purpose. Monsieur de Barras was vigilant and audacious, and never missed an opportunity of securing a private interview, even though but a momentary one. It happened one evening that Rhoda was writing in the room which had formerly been the scene of her studies under the direction of Mademoiselle de Barras, and which was now her accustomed sitting-room. While she occupied this chamber, however, she always observed the precaution of keeping her maid Willett in the room. Upon this occasion she had been, as usual, in attendance, quietly pursuing her work at an humble distance, while her young mistress was writing. It was now, however, considerably past the hour at which the other inmates of the house usually retired to rest, and relying upon this circumstance, in the full confidence of the impossibility of being disturbed, she despatched her attendant for a book to her own apartment. Willett departed, and her mistress remained alone.

The door, which the maid had closed at her departure, had not been two minutes shut, when it was re-opened, not by Willett, but, to the young lady's consternation, by Monsieur de Barras. Redolent of tobacco-smoke, his face flushed, and his eyes brilliant with wine, he swaggered into the apartment, swinging the door fast behind him as he did so, and, with a libertine smile, far more alarming than the most unequivocal menace, approached her—

"Sir—Monsieur de Barras"—stammered she, rising and advancing with a mingled emotion of anger and fear—"this is my apartment; you have made a mistake."

"A mistake!" he answered, in his own language. "By my faith, no such thing, pretty little ingrate; but quite the reverse. Now what do you wager there is not another creature living who would term so judicious and agreeable a manœuvre by so unworthy a name? No, no; impudent and wicked, *very* wicked, it may be—ha, ha—but faith the thing is no *mistake*."

"Monsieur de Barras, I really request—I must insist"— she began, retreating involuntarily a step or two, and growing every moment more and more angry and alarmed.

"Ay, ay—to be sure you must," he retorted, with an odious grin and a leer. "Request and insist, and insist and request— *helas!* what a deal of fuss and flutter these timid little birds make when one has netted them."

"I do not know, sir, what you mean—by what right—on what pretence you presume," she again began, with irrepressible indignation.

"There, there—gently—gently, gently," cried the imperturbable rascal, with a coaxing leer, as he approached her still more nearly. "Why, little rogue, what on earth are you afraid of? Am I so devilish ugly, or ill-shaped? Nonsense, child—nonsense. Come, you must not, you won't be so ill-natured."

"Monsieur de Barras, you really must leave this room," she said, in a tone more deprecatory, as her alarm increased. "If you won't go, I must—indeed I must, sir——"

"Bah! child—no such thing," he replied, roughly. "I am not such a dangerous fellow, I assure you—not I. Can't a man admire a pretty girl, without meaning her a mischief, eh?"

"I—really, monsieur—pray—I entreat of you, sir——"

"You are a pretty little rogue, and you know it," said he, relapsing into his original strain of languishing playfulness, and drawing near, with his arms extended, to prevent the possibility of her escaping.

"Sir," said she, dreading to show how really terrified she was, "this is insolence—unmanly—insufferable. Let me pass, sir—let me pass. You are no gentleman, sir, or you could not commit so gross a rudeness."

His countenance darkened perceptibly, and for the first time something of undisguised menace appeared in his manner and aspect.

"Come, come—no nonsense—what the devil rudeness do you speak of?" said he. "*Damme!* am I threatening you, pray, that you talk at this rate? I really don't understand you, Miss Rhoda."

As he said this, he sat down carelessly upon the table, keeping his eyes fixed upon her, until gradually the sterner expression which his countenance had just worn melted away once more into the confident and languishing leer with which he had first alarmed her.

"My faith!—you spoil my rest, Miss Rhoda," he resumed, with a theatrical sigh, and an odious smile. "On the honour of a gentleman, I lie awake half the night, tumbling and tossing in a fever; and then, what dreams! Come, shall I tell you my dreams?"

To her infinite delight, Rhoda at this moment heard a step traversing the passage.

"Willett! Willett!" she called, as loudly as she could.

"What are you crying about? who is harming you, you little fool; and how do you know that I will let her in?" cried de Barras, jumping briskly on the floor.

He was anticipated, however; for the door was opened before he could reach it, and not Willett, but Mrs. Marston, or, as we shall continue to call her, "mademoiselle," entered the room. Her beautiful and expressive face was pale as marble, and its whiteness, which extended even to the lips, was enhanced by the brilliant hues of the night-dress she wore—a loose robe of crimson cashmere, trimmed richly with fur, and gathered at the waist with careless grace by a silken cord. One or two clustering locks of her long dark hair hung in waving disorder upon her throat and shoulders. She was evidently inspired by some powerful and vindictive emotion, for her dark eyes seemed to stream actual fire as she glanced from de Barras to Rhoda, and from Rhoda again to him—her lips were closed, her nostrils dilated, and her bosom heaving. It was the form of beauty, exquisite and voluptuous, but tenanted by a spirit from the abyss of unearthly wrath and woe. For a moment her glance became fixed upon Monsieur de Barras—her frown darkened, and a faint smile lighted her countenance with a character that was almost deadly; she looked like a Nemesis, in the very execution of her fearful mission.

"Oh, mademoiselle!—oh, madam! I am glad you have come," stammered poor Rhoda, who, despite the evident wrath and perturbation of the intruder, was relieved unspeakably by her arrival. Monsieur de Barras looked embarrassed and angry, returned twice or thrice the flaming glance of the French lady, and, affecting to laugh, tossed his head, shrugged his shoulders, and, turning on his heel, took a turn up and down the room whistling; and then, turning abruptly, asked in a sharp and angry tone—

"Well; what is the matter now? what is all this about, eh?"

She made no other reply, but by raising her long taper hand, and making a gesture which expressed both grief and menace.

"Eh, tongue-tied—dumb, is she?" he said, wagging his

head angrily. "You are a _____. No matter. Why the d____ __ don't you stay in your room?"

"Go to your chamber, Rhoda—go," she said, in a low, resolute tone—little higher, indeed, than a whisper, but all the sterner on that account.

Rhoda glided almost mechanically from the room; and as she hurried noiselessly to her chamber, she still saw before her in imagination the pale, implacable apparition of vengeful beauty, that had so unexpectedly presented itself.

"Well, Alphonse!" said mademoiselle, drawing a long breath through her pearly teeth, now slightly disclosed by a strange, fixed smile—"what have you now to say?"

It is needless, of course, to mention that this conversation was conducted in French.

"What have I to say! come, who made you judge and executioner here?" he retorted, sullenly.

"Yes, yes, I see it all—your vows of reformation and penitence. Ah, yes, you meditate this second blow, Alphonse—and what am I to call you—what, but a villain," she answered, in an icy tone.

"And, if it comes to calling names, my dear, pray which of us is likely to fare the worst?" he retorted, with a sarcastic chuckle.

"You are a traitor, Alphonse, and mean to drive me to frenzy—to make me ruin us both," she answered.

"Not us both, if you please—say *yourself*, my dear!" he retorted.

"Yes—us *both*—I repeat; for *your* life depends on the continuance of all this, as well as mine. Yes, coward, you live upon my successes, and upbraid me with them after."

Monsieur de Barras made no answer to this home taunt, but by clenching his fist, which he shook with ruffianly menace—while, through his set teeth, he hissed at her those vilest indignities of vituperation, against which, even in its lost, most utterly debased, and forlorn condition, the outraged nature of fallen woman rises up in the agony—albeit, in the helplessness of despair.

She looked at him silently for a moment, with a gaze of stunned bewilderment—and then, with a short cry, she seized the massive candlestick that stood by, with the intent of hurling it at his head. Even as she made this gesture, however, her spirit changed. She cast it back from her, upon the ground, and clasping her hands over her face, cried in a tone of genuine agony—

"Oh, Alphonse! Alphonse! and this from you—from you—from you!"

"Well, well—don't be a fool, I tell you," he replied, after a sulky silence. "If you don't like what I say—why the ____ __ do you provoke me to it—what harm was I doing—what was the good of all this noise and fury?"

"Oh, Alphonse, to think that you—*you* would have said it—you, who were the cause of all—you, who sent me, forsaken, despairing, and alone, into the storms and temptations of the world. You, Alphonse, from whom I have hidden nothing—to whom I confessed all—to whom I forgave all—for your sake, I have borne terrible years, and endured this last extremity of wretchedness—and do you, after all, upbraid me!"

Upon this scene of remonstrance and recrimination we here suffer the curtain to fall.

We must now follow Mr. Marston in his solitary expedition to Dublin. When he took his place in the stage-coach, he had the whole interior of the vehicle to himself—and thus continued to be its solitary occupant for several miles. The coach, however, was eventually hailed, brought to, and the door being opened, Dr. Danvers got in, and took his place opposite to the passenger already established there. The worthy man was so busied in directing the disposition of his luggage, from the window, and in arranging the sundry small parcels with which he was charged, that he did not recognise his companion until they were in motion. When he did so, it was with no very pleasurable feeling—and it is probable that Marston, too, would have gladly escaped the coincidence which thus reduced them once more to the temporary necessity of a *tête-à-tête*. Embarrassing as each felt the situation to be, there was, however, no avoiding it, and after a recognition, and a few forced attempts at conversation, they became, by mutual consent, silent and uncommunicative.

The journey, though in point of space a mere trifle, was, in those slow coach days, a matter of fully five hours' duration—and before it was completed the sun had set, and darkness began to close. Whether it was that the descending twilight dispelled the painful constraint under which Marston had seemed to labour, or that some more purely spiritual and genial influence had gradually dissipated the repulsion and distrust with which, at first, he had shrunk from a renewal of intercourse with Dr. Danvers, he suddenly accosted him thus:—

"Doctor Danvers," said he, "I have been fifty times on the point of speaking to you—confidentially, of course—while sitting here opposite to you—what I believe I could scarcely bring myself to hint to any other man living—yet, I must tell it, and soon too—or I fear it will have told itself."

Dr. Danvers intimated his readiness to hear and advise, if desired—and Marston resumed abruptly, after a pause—

"Pray, Doctor Danvers, have you heard any stories of an odd kind—any surmises—I don't mean of a *moral* sort—for *those* I hold very cheap—to my prejudice? Indeed, I should hardly say to my *prejudice*—I mean, I ought to say—in short, have you heard people remark upon any fancied eccentricities—or that sort of thing—about me?"

He put the question with obvious difficulty, and at last seemed to overcome his own reluctance with a sort of angry and excited self-contempt and impatience. Doctor Danvers was a little puzzled by the interrogatory, and admitted, in reply, that he did not comprehend its drift.

"Doctor Danvers," he resumed, sternly and dejectedly, "I told you, in the chance interview we had some months ago, that I was haunted by a certain fear—I did not define it—nor do I think you suspect its nature—it is a fear of nothing mortal—but a ghastly terror of the immortal tenant of this body—my *mind*, sir, is beginning to play me strange tricks—my guide mocks and terrifies me."

There was a perceptible tinge of horror in the look of astonishment with which Dr. Danvers listened.

"You are a gentleman, sir, and a Christian clergyman—what I have said, and shall say, is confided to your honour—to be held sacred as the confession of misery, and hidden from the coarse gaze of the world—I have become subject to a hideous delusion—it comes at intervals—I do not think any mortal suspects it, except, maybe, my daughter Rhoda—it comes and disappears—and comes again—I kept my pleasant secret for a long time, but at last I let it slip, and committed myself, fortunately, to but one person, and that my daughter—and, even so, I hardly think she understood me—I recollected myself before I had disclosed the grotesque and infernal chimera that haunts me."

Marston paused—he was stooped forward, and looking upon the floor of the vehicle, so that his companion could not see his countenance—a silence ensued, which was interrupted by Marston, who once more resumed—

"Sir," said he, "I know not *why*, but I *have* longed—intensely longed—for some trustworthy ear, into which to pour this horrid secret—*why*, I repeat, I cannot tell—for I expect no sympathy, and hate compassion. It is, I suppose, the restless nature of the devil that is in me—but, be it what it may, I will speak to you—but to *you* only—for the present, at least, to you alone."

Doctor Danvers again assured him that he might repose the most entire confidence in his secrecy.

"The human mind, I take it, must have either comfort in the past, or hope in the future," he continued, "otherwise, it is in *danger*; to me, sir, the past is intolerably repulsive—one boundless, barren, and hideous golgotha of dead hopes and murdered opportunities—the future, still blacker and more furious, peopled with dreadful features of horror and menace, and losing itself in utter darkness. Sir, I do not exaggerate—between such a past, and such a future, I stand upon this miserable present—and the only comfort I still am capable of feeling, is that no human being pities me—that I stand aloof from the insults of compassion, and the hypocrisies of sympathetic morality—and that I can safely defy all the respectable scoundrels in Christendom to enhance, by one feather's weight, the load which I myself have accumulated, and which I myself hourly and unaided sustain."

Doctor Danvers here introduced a word or two in the direction of their former conversation.

"No, sir, there is no comfort from that quarter either," said Marston, bitterly, "you but cast your seeds, as the parable terms your teaching, upon the barren sea, in wasting them on me. My fate, be it what it may, is as irrevocably fixed as though I were dead and judged a hundred years ago."

"This cursed dream," he resumed, abruptly, "that every

day enslaves me more and more, has reference to that—that *occurrence* about Wynston Berkley—he is the hero of the hellish illusion. At certain times, sir, it seems to me, as if he, though dead, were still invested with a sort of spurious life—going about unrecognised, except by me, in squalor and contempt—and whispering away, with thrilling slanders, my fame and life—labouring with the malignant industry of a fiend, to involve me in the meshes of that special perdition, from which alone I shrink, and to which this emissary of hell seems to have predestined me. Sir, this is a monstrous and hideous extravagance—a delusion—but, after all, no more than a trick of the *imagination*—the reason, the judgment, is untouched—I cannot choose but *see* all the damned phantasmagoria—but I do not believe it real—and this is the difference between my case—and—and—*madness*."

They were now entering the suburbs of Dublin—and Dr. Danvers, pained and shocked beyond measure by this unlooked-for disclosure, and not knowing what remark or comfort to offer, relieved his temporary embarrassment by looking from the window, as though attracted by the flash of the lamps—among which the vehicle was now moving. Marston, however, laid his hand upon his arm, and thus recalled him, for a moment, to a forced attention.

"It must seem strange to you, Doctor, that I should trust this cursed secret to your keeping," he said—"and, truth to say, it seems so to myself—I cannot account for the impulse, the irresistible power of which has forced me to disclose the hateful mystery to you—but the fact is this—beginning like a speck—this one idea has gradually darkened and dilated, until it has filled my entire mind—the solitary consciousness of the gigantic mastery it has established there, had grown intolerable—I must have told it—the sense of solitude under this aggressive and tremendous delusion, was agony, hourly death to my soul—that is the secret of my talkativeness—my sole excuse for plaguing you with the dreams of a wretched hypochondriac."

Dr. Danvers assured him that no apologies were needed, and was only restrained from adding the expression of that pity which he really felt, by the fear of irritating a temper so full of bitterness, pride, and defiance. A few minutes more, and the coach having reached its destination, they bid one another farewell, and parted.

At that time there resided in a decent mansion, in one of the northern suburbs of Dublin, a dapper little gentleman whom we shall call Dr. Parkes. This gentleman was the proprietor and sole professional manager of a private asylum for the insane, and enjoyed a high reputation, and a proportionate amount of business, in his melancholy calling. It was about the second day after the conversation we have just sketched, that this little gentleman having visited, according to his custom, all his domestic patients, was about to take his accustomed walk in his somewhat restricted pleasure-grounds, when his servant announced a visitor.

"A gentleman," he repeated; "you have seen him before—eh?"

"No, sir," replied the man; "he is in the study, sir."

"Ha!—a *professional* call. Well, we shall see."

So saying, the little gentleman summoned his gravest look, and hastened to the chamber of audience.

On entering he found a man dressed well, but gravely, having in his air and manner something of high-breeding. In countenance striking, dark-featured, and stern, furrowed with the lines of pain or thought, rather than of age, although his dark hairs were largely mingled with white.

The physician bowed, and requested the stranger to take

a chair; he, however, nodded slightly and impatiently, as if to intimate an intolerance of ceremony, and, advancing a step or two, said abruptly—

"My name, sir, is Marston; I have come to give you a patient."

The doctor bowed with a still deeper inclination, and paused for a continuance of the communication thus auspiciously commenced.

"You are Dr. Parkes, I take it for granted," said Marston, in the same tone.

"Your most obedient, humble servant, sir," replied he, with the polite formality of the day, and another grave bow.

"Doctor," demanded Marston, fixing his eye upon him sternly, and significantly tapping his own forehead, "can you stay execution?"

The physician looked puzzled, hesitated, and at last requested his visitor to be more explicit.

"Can you," said Marston, with the same slow and stern articulation, and after a considerable pause—"can you *prevent* the malady you profess to cure?—can you meet and defeat the enemy half way?—can you scare away the spirit of madness *before* it takes actual possession, and while it is still only hovering about its threatened victim?"

"Sir," he replied, "in certain cases—in very many, indeed—the enemy, as you well call it, *may* thus be met, and effectually worsted at a distance. Timely interposition, in ninety cases out of a hundred, is *everything*; and, I assure you, I hear your question with much pleasure, inasmuch as I assume it to have reference to the case of the patient about whom you desire to consult me; and who is, therefore, I hope, as yet merely *menaced* with the misfortune from which you would save him."

"I, myself, am that patient, sir," said Marston, with an

effort; "your surmise is right. I am not mad, but unequivocally and awfully menaced with madness; it is not to be mistaken. Sir, there is no misunderstanding the tremendous and intolerable signs that glare upon my mind."

"And pray, sir, have you consulted your friends or your family upon the course best to be pursued?" inquired Dr. Parkes, with grave interest.

"No, sir," he answered sharply and almost fiercely; "I have no fancy to make myself the subject of a writ *de lunatico inquirendo*; I don't want to lose my liberty and my property at a blow. The course I mean to take has been advised by no one but myself—is *known* to no other. I now disclose it, and the causes of it, to you, a gentleman, and my professional adviser, in the expectation that you will guard with the strictest secrecy my spontaneous revelations—this you promise me?"

"Certainly, Mr. Marston; I have neither the disposition nor the right to withhold such a promise," answered the physician.

"Well, then, I will first tell you the arrangement I purpose, with your permission, to make, and then I shall answer all your questions respecting my own case," resumed Marston, gloomily. "I wish to place myself under your care, to live under your roof, reserving my full liberty of action. I must be free to come and to go as I will; and on the other hand, I undertake that you shall find me an amenable and docile patient enough. In addition, I stipulate that there shall be no attempt whatever made to communicate with those who are connected with me: these terms agreed upon, I place myself in your hands. You will find in me, as I said before, a deferential patient, and I trust not a troublesome one. I hope you will excuse my adding, that I shall myself pay the charge of my sojourn here from week to week, in advance."

The proposed arrangement was a strange one; and

although Dr. Parkes dimly foresaw some of the embarrass-
ments which might possibly arise from his accepting it, there
was yet so much that was reasonable as well as advantageous
in the proposal, that he could not bring himself to decline it.

The preliminary arrangement concluded, Dr. Parkes
proceeded to his more strictly professional investigation. It
is, of course, needless to recapitulate the details of Marston's
tormenting fancies, with which the reader has indeed been
already sufficiently acquainted. Dr. Parkes, having attentively
listened to the narrative, and satisfied himself as to the
physical health of his patient, was still sorely puzzled as to
the probable issue of the awful struggle already but too
obviously commenced between the mind and its destroyer in
the strange case before him. One satisfactory symptom
unquestionably was, the as yet transitory nature of the
delusion, and the evident and energetic tenacity with which
reason contended for her vital ascendancy. It was a case,
however, which for many reasons sorely perplexed him, but
of which, notwithstanding, he was disposed, whether rightly
or wrongly the reader will speedily see, to take by no means
a decidedly gloomy view.

Having disburthened his mind of this horrible secret,
Marston felt for a time a sense of relief amounting almost to
elation. With far less of apprehension and dismay than he
had done so for months before, he that night repaired to his
bedroom. There was nothing in his case, Dr. Parkes believed,
to warrant his keeping any watch upon Marston's actions,
and accordingly he bid him good-night, in the full confidence
of meeting him, if not better, at least not worse, on the
ensuing morning.

He miscalculated, however. Marston had probably
himself been conscious of some coming crisis in his hideous
malady, when he took the decisive step of placing himself

under the care of Dr. Parkes. Certain it is, that upon that very night the disease broke forth in a new and appalling development. Dr. Parkes, whose bedroom was next to that occupied by Marston, was awakened in the dead of the night by a howling, more like that of a beast than a human voice, and which gradually swelled into an absolute yell; then came some horrid laughter and entreaties, thick and frantic; then again the same unearthly howl. The practised ear of Dr. Parkes recognised but too surely the terrific import of those sounds. Springing from his bed, and seizing the candle which always burned in his chamber, in anticipation of such sudden and fearful emergencies, he hurried with a palpitating heart, and spite of his long habituation to such scenes as he expected, with a certain sense of horror, to the chamber of his aristocratic patient.

Late as it was, Marston had not yet gone to bed; his candle was still burning, and he himself, half dressed, stood in the centre of the floor, his sword grasped in his hand, all shaking, and livid with terror and rage—and his eyes burning with the preterhuman fires of insanity. As Doctor Parkes entered the chamber, another shout, or rather yell, thundered from the lips of this demoniac effigy; and the mad-doctor stood freezing with horror in the doorway, and yet exerting what remained to him of presence of mind, in the vain endeavour, in the flaring light of the candle, to catch and fix with his own practised eye the terrific gaze of the maniac. Second after second, and minute after minute, he stood confronting this frightful slave of Satan, in the momentary expectation that he would close with and destroy him. On a sudden, however, this brief agony of suspense was terminated—a change like an awaking consciousness of realities, or rather like the withdrawal of some hideous and visible influence from within, passed over the tense and darkened features of the wretched being—a look of horrified perplexity, doubt, and inquiry, he turned from object to object, and at last said, in a subdued and sullen tone, to Dr. Parkes—

"Who are you, sir? What do you want here? Who are you, sir, I say?"

"Who am I? Why, your physician, sir—Doctor Parkes, sir—the owner of this house, sir," replied he, with all the sternness he could command, and yet white as a spectre with agitation. "For shame, sir—for shame—to give way thus. What do you mean by creating this causeless alarm, and disturbing the whole household at so unseasonable an hour? For shame, sir—go to your bed; undress yourself this moment—for shame."

Doctor Parkes, as he spoke, was reassured by the arrival of one of his servants, alarmed by the unmistakable sounds of violent frenzy; he signed, however, to the man not to enter, feeling confident, as he did, that the paroxysm had spent itself.

"Ay, ay," muttered Marston, looking almost sheepishly; "Dr. Parkes, to be sure. What was I thinking of; how cursedly absurd! And this," he continued, glancing at his sword, which he threw impatiently upon a sofa as he spoke. "Folly—nonsense! A false alarm, as you say, Doctor. I beg your pardon."

As Marston spoke, he proceeded with much agitation slowly to undress himself. He had, however, but commenced the process, when, turning abruptly to Doctor Parkes, he said, with a countenance of horror, and in a whisper—

"By _____, doctor, it has been upon me worse than ever. I would have sworn I had the villain with me for hours—*hours*, sir—torturing me with his damned sneering threats; till, by _____, I could stand it no longer, and took my sword. Oh, doctor, doctor—my God, my God—can't you save me; can nothing be done for me?"

Pale, covered with the dews of horror, he uttered these last words in accents of such imploring despair, as might have borne across the dreadful gulph the prayer of Dives for that one drop of water which was never to cool his burning tongue.

Upon the night on which we last saw the guilty and unhappy household of Dunoran, the interview which we described being concluded, Eugenie returned to her solitude, leaving Monsieur de Barras in a somewhat inflamed temper, to the solitary enjoyment of his moody and unprofitable meditations. He was much too angry and too excited to think of sleep. He sate, for fully half-an-hour, muttering, with folded arms and a flushed and defiant countenance. He then got up, and having repaired to his own private apartment, there regaled himself with tobacco and brandy, until his uncomfortable feelings gave place to a happier train of dreamy reverie. There, with cravat removed and vest unbuttoned, we leave him, quaffing his favourite nectar, and wreathed in his narcotic clouds, in all the majestic luxury of a newly-translated demigod.

Rhoda had retired to her own room, accompanied by her faithful maid, Willett. There in the darkened chamber, lying in her sleepless bed, and longing for day, she might easily have counted the deep respirations of her profoundly unconscious attendant, sleeping soundly in the same apartment, and the loud throbbing of her own fluttered heart. Hour after hour passed away, each successively finding her more keenly and excitedly vigilant than its predecessor. At last she heard a stealthy sound at the door. The bolt cautiously revolved, and Monsieur de Barras's head, partially illumined by a shaded candle, was furtively introduced. He was obviously heated with "strong drink," and his odious face, inflamed with insolence and sensuality, appeared to her more appalling than could the most ghastly chimera of a nightmare, had it approached her in embodied and substantial shape.

This hated and dreaded form advanced, holding his breath, and on tip-toe, toward the bed where she lay. With a sudden effort, mastering the terrible fascination which held her, she started upright in her bed, and screamed in an agony of terror for Willett. The rustling in Willett's bed, and the addition of her voice, in an under key, to that which had greeted his entrance, arrested the progress of Monsieur de Barras. He had evidently not calculated upon the presence of the attendant. Muttering some incoherent words implying that he had mistaken the apartment, and interspersing these broken sentences with abundance of suppressed but genuine imprecations, he hastily withdrew, and Willett promptly secured the door against the possibility of a renewed invasion.

This outrage was quite enough to determine Rhoda to adopt a course respecting which she had been long hesitating. Early next morning, attended by Willett, she glided from the sombre mansion, once her happy home, now grown unutterably terrible to her, and unimpeded and unsuspected, hurried in indescribable trepidation down the great avenue; keeping as she went as much under the cover of the ample rows of timber as was possible, she yet scarcely ventured to pause or look behind her, until she had passed the great gate, and entered the public road.

The reader will probably have anticipated us, when we relate that she held her way direct to Newton Park; and, on reaching the hall-door, requested the surprised domestic to inform Mrs. Mervyn that Miss Marston had taken the liberty of calling, and was most anxious to see her immediately.

"My dear young friend," said the kind lady, as soon as she

had listened to poor Rhoda's narrative to its close, "I can scarcely describe the gratification with which I see you here—the happiness with which I welcome you to Newton Park; nor, indeed, the anxiety with which I constantly contemplated your trying and painful position at Dunoran. Indeed I ought to be angry with you for having refused me this happiness so long—but you have made amends at last; though, indeed, it was impossible to have deferred it longer. You must not fancy, however, that I will consent to lose you so soon as you seem to have intended. No, no—I have found it too hard to catch you, to let you take wing so easily; beside, I have others to consult as well as myself, and persons, too, who are just as anxious as I am to make a prisoner of you here."

The good Mrs. Mervyn accompanied these words with looks so sly, and emphasis so significant, that Rhoda was fain to look down, to hide her blushes; and compassionating the confusion she herself had caused, the kind old lady led her with her to the chamber which was henceforward, as long as she consented to remain, to be her own apartment.

How that day was passed, and how fleetly its hours sped away, it is needless to tell. Old Mervyn had his gentle as well as his grim aspect; and no welcome was ever more cordial and tender than that with which he greeted the unprotected child of his unsocial and repulsive neighbour. It would be impossible to convey any idea of the manifold and important confidences which, after the manner of young ladies, the two pretty girls—Rhoda and Emily Howard—had mutually to make after their long separation. Nor need we describe the countless assiduities and the secret delight with which young Mervyn attended their rambles.

The party were assembled at supper. What a contrast did this cheerful, happy—unutterably happy—gathering, present in the mind of Rhoda, to the dull, drear, fearful evenings which she had long been wont to pass at Dunoran.

As they sate together in cheerful and happy intercourse, a chaise drove up to the hall-door, and the knocking had hardly ceased to reverberate, when a well-known voice was audible in the hall.

Young Mervyn started to his feet, and merrily ejaculating, "Charles Marston!—this is delightful!" disappeared, and in an instant returned with Charles himself.

We pass over all the embraces of brother and sister—the tears and smiles of re-united affection. We omit the cordial shaking of hands—the kind looks of all—the tender looks of some—the questions and answers—all these, and all the little attentions of that good old-fashioned hospitality, which was never weary of demonstrating the cordiality of its welcome—we abandon to the imagination of the kind reader. After the first hilarious expansion of all the genial feelings called into play by an unexpected and welcome arrival had subsided, it speedily became manifest that Charles Marston was depressed, or, at all events, perplexed by some pressing care or anxiety. His countenance, and more than even his looks—the fitful intervals of abstraction which interrupted his conversation, and evidenced his unconsciousness of what was passing about him—betrayed the urgency of this untold, and, as it seemed, painfully engrossing anxiety.

It was, therefore, with more of curiosity than surprise, that they heard Charles, after one of these fits of abstraction, abruptly ask old Mr. Mervyn to favour him with a few minutes' conversation, respecting a subject upon which he greatly desired his advice. With a ready assent the old gentleman arose, and led the way to his study.

"My dear sir," said Marston, as soon as they were seated and the door closed, "I do not know whether I ought to rejoice or to grieve at the strange and agitating information which has reached me. It is strange, shocking, but, at the same time, in a certain respect, most satisfactory. You will judge. It is now a few months since I received an anonymous letter, in which the writer, after strongly inveighing against Mademoiselle de Barras, declared that he was about, at an early day, to unfold to me such a train of villainy and imposture upon her part, as would involve, perhaps, the necessity of placing her in the dock, to stand her trial for felony. Little good-will had I any reason, as you know, to bear towards Mademoiselle de Barras (for so I shall call her), yet this letter shocked and pained me. I felt, however, that I had no choice in the matter, and that I ought not to withhold from my father the fact that such a letter had reached me. I accordingly wrote, and received from him an answer so intemperate and so strange, that I resolved not again to allude to the subject, unless it was forced upon me in such an unequivocal and fully substantiated way as to demand investigation and ulterior proceedings. Well, sir, this *has* come to pass. A little more than a fortnight previously to my leaving Cambridge, I received a second letter from the same anonymous hand, enlarging, in matter of detail, upon the first, and promising further and more authenticated information. This was, a few days later, followed by a third, merely promising, in a few lines, an interview with the writer, and this time bearing the signature in full of 'John Crane.' This John Crane accordingly called upon me in my chambers, and judge yourself of the nature and effect of his communication."

Charles Marston then proceeded to detail what had passed between them, Mervyn listening meanwhile with the profoundest attention.

"And where is this John Crane?" inquired Mervyn, as soon

as the strange narrative was concluded.

"I have brought him with me," answered young Marston. "I called here for the purpose of consulting you before going to Dunoran, as I am really agitated as to what course I ought to pursue."

"Well," said Mervyn, "it strikes me that this occurrence is a most fortunate one for you and for your sister, and indeed, I may add, for Mr. Marston himself. The effect of it must be to dissever a connexion which has been the curse of your family. Your father fancies me his enemy. I cannot disabuse his mind, but you will believe me when I say, that so far from wishing him ill, my earnest desire is to see him occupying the position which he ought to fill—to see him disenthralled from a bondage at once so degrading, and so grievous to be borne. I speak frankly to you, my young friend, and know you will not take offence at my plain expressions. Your father is a hot-tempered, and, I fear, an implacable man, and I have little hope of our ever being upon terms of pleasant intercourse; but, although he has once or twice succeeded in making me a little angry, I bear him no grudge; and thus far I believe you will bear me out."

"Indeed, my dear sir, I well know it," replied Charles, "and that I do so is proved, if no otherwise, by my consulting you upon a matter so nearly concerning his dearest interests, and throwing them and my own conduct entirely into your hands. Do, therefore, my dear and honoured friend, give me, freely and without fear of misconstruction, your advice in this painful and difficult emergency."

Mervyn mused for a time, and then observed—

"I think it very fortunate that your father happens to be absent just now. It was his intention to have met you, and returned in your company from Dublin; he will, therefore, probably not continue long from home; and it appears to me advisable in the highest degree that the crisis of this affair should have taken place before his return."

"The crisis! Then you think it necessary to proceed upon the information I have received?" asked Charles.

"Undoubtedly," replied Mr. Mervyn; "there is no honest alternative; you cannot do otherwise. I will myself take the information of this witness, John Crane—make out a warrant, and arrest the Frenchwoman to-night; and we can send her back to gaol in the chaise which brought you hither."

There was in the stern promptitude with which Mervyn proposed to act, something repulsive to the feelings of the younger man—something almost terrible. A few minutes' reflection, however, satisfied him that, sooner or later, such a step must be taken; and, as the procedure was inevitable, the desirableness of despatch, for every reason, was apparent.

"How did this John Crane come to be cognizant of the facts?" inquired Mervyn, pursuing the train of his own reflections.

"He was in Sir Wynston Berkley's service when he was at Rouen, where he formed an acquaintance with Mademoiselle de Barras," answered Marston, "and afterwards he was for nearly a year a servant in an English family resident in the same neighbourhood, where mademoiselle was subsequently domesticated as governess. But it was long previously to this that he witnessed the important event; and here, too, was received from Mademoiselle de Barras that injury, which, if I mistake not, he now seeks to avenge."

"Ay, ay," said Mervyn—"wheel within wheel—complication of motive and relation, as usual; and this injury was——"

"Why, as he supposes, having her own reasons for removing him," answered Charles, "she managed, without his discovering, or even suspecting her share in the matter—until within a few months since, he heard all in a chance interview with an old fellow-servant—she contrived, as I say, without appearing in the matter, to have his honesty suspected, and he was discharged in consequence without a character; and there, as I suspect, lies the whole motive of his conduct. The unhappy connexion with my father he learned from one of the late Sir Wynston's servants, whom he had known in France."

"His story is, however, consistent, whatever may be his motive," observed Mervyn. "If he forswears himself, he does so at his own proper peril—we must receive, and act upon his sworn deposition. As for you, I think it will be well, in order to avoid exciting their suspicion, that you should at once proceed to Dunoran. They will, unquestionably, soon hear of your arrival here—if, indeed, they have not already done so—and, in the process of their inquiries, goodness knows what other circumstances may come to their ears. Your witness, for instance, may have been talking amongst the servants. Do you, therefore, proceed to Dunoran as speedily as you may. I will see to all the rest, and follow as soon as preparations are completed."

As Charles was hurrying from Mr. Mervyn's study, intending, without again joining the party in the supper-room, to set out forthwith for Dunoran, he was encountered accidentally in the hall by Willett. With a kind but hurried greeting he was about to pass her, when one or two expressions which escaped her in her voluble welcome, touching her young mistress, fixed his attention and arrested his progress. Once engaged upon such a theme, it may easily be imagined he did not leave her until he had extracted from her a recital, inflamed with countless exaggerations, after the manner of such narrators, of the insolence to which his sister had been subjected by Monsieur de Barras.

Such a narrative, it may easily be conceived, did not tend much to mitigate the feelings, or to calm the excitement with which he might naturally have been supposed to approach the inmates of Dunoran. From his father he had inherited a fiery and somewhat haughty temper, and his pride and his indignation were incensed to the uttermost at the idea of the insult which had been offered to his beloved and unprotected sister, in her own home, by this audacious French parasite. Snuffing the night air angrily, and with rapid strides, he traversed the sombre interval of ancient woodland which interposed between Newton Park and the desolate mansion-house of Dunoran. His mind agitated and engrossed by these energetic and stormy emotions, he was scarcely conscious of the interval he had passed when he found himself under the shadow of its melancholy and neglected walls.

Without giving any summons, he turned the latch-pin, moveable, as in many Irish country houses, from the outside. Neither bar nor bolt secured the door as yet; and pushing it open, he stood alone, and unperceived, in the solemn shadow of the old hall. Here he paused for a moment. There was in his peculiar situation something so unwonted and even horrible, that a sense of awe overcame him, and he felt as an avenging spectre, stealing by night, unfelt and unseen, through old familiar scenes upon its preternatural mission, might be fancied to do. He passed on to the inner hall; a door opening from it was ajar, and a light shone through the aperture. Charles Marston entered, and found himself alone with the handsome Frenchwoman.

She started, and changed colour. Perhaps the awkwardness of Rhoda's absence, and the difficulty of accounting for it satisfactorily, disconcerted her; or, it may be, one of those mysterious and ominous misgivings, portending unknown and undefined disaster, agitated her soul; or perhaps, again, there was that in Marston's countenance which spoke of danger. She looked in his face with a gloomy surprise, and coldly said—

"Mr. Marston is in Dublin, and we did not expect you to-night. Your arrival is unlooked for; but whatever you require, you can have."

And so saying, she rang the bell, and again fixed her full dark eyes anxiously upon him.

Spite of all his sense of right, Charles Marston felt a certain commotion and sickening of the heart, as he looked upon the fated, forlorn, and guilty being, upon whose defenceless head a storm so irresistibly awful was about to burst.

"I require nothing—nothing at present," he said, in subdued and hurried accents.

A long pause ensued, in which the servant came and went—an ominous and painful interval.

"Where is my sister?" asked he, abruptly, and with the unacknowledged design, it may be, of forcing his mind into a channel less painful than the compunctious and half-relenting one into which it was insensibly gliding.

"She is gone to visit a friend," answered 'Madame,' with a perceptible change of colour; and while she spoke, as fortune would have it, Monsieur de Barras swaggered lazily into the room.

The sight of this ruffian, doubly hateful from all he had lately learned of him—presented at the very moment, too, when the image of his insulted sister had risen before his mind—the sister whom his unmanly insolence had driven from the house, whose comforts and command he was now coolly usurping—this provoking apparition was seasonably presented, and in a moment all the fierce and angry emotions which Charles at first experienced, had rushed back with a fury a hundredfold intensified.

"Ah!—*parbleu*—Master Charles, himself, I suppose!" ejaculated he, in his native tongue, at the same time throwing himself carelessly into a chair, and eyeing the young man with supercilious familiarity.

"Where is my sister, and for what cause has she left the house?" he re-iterated, in a tone which showed how fearfully his wrath had been kindled at sight of the easy Frenchman.

"Answer him—why don't you answer him, *ma sœur?*" said Monsieur de Barras, carelessly.

"*Sister!*—how dare you call madame there your sister?" said Marston, sternly.

Monsieur de Barras started perceptibly, and darted a frightened glance of inquiry at the Frenchwoman. She stood motionless as a figure of stone, and so deadly pale, that she appeared on the very point of fainting.

"Yes," cried Marston, fiercely, "your looks betray you. *Sister*, indeed! abominable, degraded impostor!"

"Why, what do you mean? a hundred thousand devils, what do you mean, Monsieur?" cried the Frenchman, assuming the tone and swagger of a bully.

"You *know* what I mean, dog!—Madame there knows what I mean," thundered Charles, losing all command of himself, "she is not your sister—she is your WIFE."

"My—my—my wife?" faltered de Barras, with a corpse-like visage.

"Ay, your wife—your *wife*; mean, pitiful scoundrel," cried Charles.

"Why, how is this?—what do you say?—wife, wife, indeed! My faith! the young gentleman has strange dreams," said Mademoiselle, rallying a little, with an effort, and affecting to laugh, but looking ghastly as death.

"Don't fancy that you can maintain the vile cheat one hour longer," persisted the young man; "man and wife you two are—man and wife; and I can prove it, and will prove it, too, where proof will have its proper weight. I have not come unprovided with testimony; I have a witness with me—one whom you well remember—whose name will confound you—the servant who himself witnessed the ceremony. You cannot pretend to forget John Crane, who, at your own desire, witnessed the marriage: he is with me; I have brought him here; and we shall soon see whether his testimony is worthy of credit or not."

Mademoiselle de Barras attempted to speak—cleared her voice, and again attempted it; but all her wonted presence of mind, her practised coolness and courage, forsook her, and she trembled violently, merely repeating, after an interval, in a gasping whisper, "*Mon Dieu! mon Dieu!*"

"And you, sir—not Monsieur de Barras"—pursued Charles, with bitter and furious scorn, "but Monsieur Rocqueville, as I am informed—you, detestable, abject scoundrel, you have dared to insult my sister, Miss Marston, in her own home, and to force her to seek an asylum in the house of a stranger. Execrable poltroon! what can you answer to this charge?"

"*Ma foi!*" cried the Frenchman, setting his arms akimbo, while his countenance wore that worst of characters, a mixture of livid fear and fury; "here is a pretty piece of work, and all got up by a fool of a coxcomb. Psha! the girl knows what she is about, and was glad of an excuse to throw herself into young Monsieur Mervyn's arms."

The cool insolence of this reply transported Marston to such a pitch of fury, that, forgetting every consideration in his sense of outrage and audacity, he collared the rascal, and struck him, with his whole force, twice in the face with his clenched hand. He staggered, nearly stunned, against the wall, and recovering himself, half drew his sword, but returned it with vehemence to its scabbard, and slunk muttering from the room, the very type of a cowed and malignant bully. With the disappearance of this wretch, Charles Marston's furious excitement subsided, and he looked round the room like one newly awakened from a fit of delirium. He felt a painful revulsion as his eye lighted upon the form of the young, the lost and miserable being, whose destruction was now inevitably drawing near. He turned and stood in the doorway, with his face averted. After a few moments of silence, he heard a slight rustling behind him, and a hand was laid upon his arm. He looked round— Mademoiselle was gazing up into his face, with a look so wan, so imploring and woe-begone, that he felt a pang of pity, almost of fear, stir his heart. This look of mute, agonised entreaty, was fixed on him for many seconds, and then without one word spoken, the wretched and guilty woman glided to a sofa, sate down, and covered her face with her hands.

Oppressed with a strange and horrible conflict of feelings, he hurried silently from her presence, resolved to stay the execution of the warrant until the morning, and himself to escape the harrowing spectacle.

With feelings very different from those with which he had approached the house, he now emerged into the chill night air, and pursued his solitary way under the airy vaulting of the solemn and densely dark trees; and, ever as he went, he seemed to hear the rustling sound behind him—to feel the light pressure on his arm—and to see the death-like features, and full, earnest eyes of the doomed Frenchwoman, upturned to his face.

He felt the inevitability of the measure about to be taken— his reason acknowledged alike its necessity and its justice. He saw too that, morally, he would himself be accessory to an abominable and flagitious imposture, if he suppressed the evidence, which it was impossible to make public without the destruction of the fallen woman, for whom, spite of everything, he could not divest his mind of some sentiment of compassion.

It was now arranged that on the next morning the guilty woman should be arrested, and Charles Marston laid his throbbing head upon the pillow that night in great perturbation and excitement.

When the grey light of morning visited his sleepless eyes, Charles Marston rose, sorely troubled in mind—filled with new anxieties and alarms—foremost among which was the conjecture that his father might, in the interval, have haply returned, and that, in the wayward and ungoverned burst of fury too likely to be evoked in the coming collision, he might commit some act of crime or violence which would fatally compromise himself.

Mr. Mervyn, more than ever impressed with the importance (as regarded the interests, prospects, and position of his young friends in whose welfare he took so keen an interest) of successfully conducting the painful but necessary measures which he himself had advised, determined that no conventional obstacles of false delicacy should stand in the way of what he regarded as a duty, and an act of mercy to an abused and injured family, and himself accompanied the party, who proceeded to Dunoran upon this unwonted and disagreeable mission.

It was a dreary, misty, ominous morning, and, brushing the moisture from the withered grass, Charles Marston paced and repaced the space which lay under the wall of the gate-house of Newton Park, awaiting, in agitated suspense, the return of the little party whose departure he had so lately witnessed.

Twenty times did he consult his watch, and listen

breathlessly for the sound of their return; more and more painful, minute after minute, did his suspense become. At length, when nearly twice the interval on which he had calculated had actually expired, he heard the rumble and grinding of the chaise wheels rapidly approaching. His first impulse was to run forward and anticipate its arrival—his next was to draw further back from the entrance, and postpone, if possible, the scene which was now so painfully imminent. With a beating heart and pale face, he awaited the approaching disclosure. The vehicle stopped, and Mr. Mervyn alone got out.

"Egad, Charles, they have stolen a march upon us; they left the place together last night, not an hour after your visit," said Mr. Mervyn.

"She has escaped, then?" said Charles.

"Ay, ay, the demirep—she has got the start of us by ten good hours," replied he.

"Thank God!" said Charles, mechanically, and drawing a deep sigh.

"Hey! egad, I suspect you're a blockhead, sir," said old Mervyn, testily.

Marston hastened to appease the worthy old gentleman's irritation, by a profusion of thanks and acknowledgements for his kindness and advice.

"Well, well," said he, "the thing can't be helped; so let us dismiss it, at all events, for the present, and get home to our breakfast."

And, so saying, he placed his arm in that of the young man, and they walked together to the house.

Mademoiselle de Barras was indeed the wife of Rocqueville— married but to be cast off and forsaken by the villain whom she had loved with something like idolatry. Thrown upon the world, with a heart fired with resentment, and wrung with sorrow, she had yielded up her soul to the darkest passions and the wildest grief. For years she had neither seen nor heard of him, and for years the struggling emotions of sorrow, fierce resentment, and unavailing love, maintained her, in the absence of higher and better influences, against the assaults of those constant temptations to which, in a dissolute age, her extreme beauty, and now unprotected condition, exposed her. Naturally ambitious and intriguing, the perilous tendencies of such a spirit had never been schooled in her by the mighty and benignant principles of religion. Of her accidental acquaintance at Rouen with Sir Wynston Berkley, and her subsequent introduction, in an evil hour, into the family at Dunoran, it is unnecessary to speak. The unhappy terms on which she found Marston living with his wife, suggested, in their mutual alienation, the idea of founding a double influence in the household; and to conceive the idea, and to act upon it, were, in her active mind, the same. Young, beautiful, fascinating, she well knew the power of her attractions, and determined, though probably without one thought of transgressing the limits of literal propriety, to bring them all to bear upon the discontented, retired roué, for whom she cared absolutely nothing, except as the instrument, and in part the victim of her schemes. Thus yielding to the double instinct that swayed her, she gratified, at the same time, her love of intrigue and her love of power. At length, however, came the hour which demanded a sacrifice to the evil influence she had hitherto worshipped on such easy terms. She found that her power must now be secured by crime, and she fell. Then came the arrival of Sir Wynston—his murder—her elopement with Marston, and, in the midst of her guilty and joyless triumph, the arrival of her husband, who, reduced, by some one of those reverses incident even to the expertest of gamesters, to destitution, bethought him at last of his wife, made inquiries, traced, followed, and found her. Her situation enabled him to command his own terms; and, strange to say, spite of his meanness, rapacity, and selfish profligacy, she still loved him. What can entirely kill the first love of a woman's heart, or what entirely disenchant the once idolized object? Thus bound together in degraded conspiracy, they lived on from day to day. At last, however, came the blow, long suspended and terrific, which shattered all their hopes and schemes, and drove them once again upon the world. She and her husband made their way unobstructed to Dublin, where they parted, and by different routes met again in London, and thence pursued their way to Paris. Arrived in the capital of France, Rocqueville speedily dissipated, in the profligate courses to which he immediately returned, whatever remained of the money and valuables which his wife had taken with her from Dunoran in her hurried flight; and Madame de Rocqueville, as she now styled herself, was glad to place herself once more as governess in an aristocratic family. So far her good fortune had prevailed in averting the punishment but too well-earned by her past life. But a day of reckoning was to come. A few years later, France was involved in the uproar and conflagration of revolution. Noble families were scattered, beggared, decimated; and their dependants, often dragged along with them into the flaming abyss, in many instances suffered the last dire extremities of human ill. It was at this awful period that a retribution so frightful and so extraordinary overtook Madame de Rocqueville, that we may hereafter be tempted to make it the subject of a separate and detailed narrative. Until then the reader will rest satisfied with what he already knows of her history; and meanwhile bid a long, and as it may possibly turn out, an eternal farewell to that beautiful embodiment of an evil and disastrous influence.

Charles Marston, with the advice of his friend, Mr.

Mervyn, resolved to lose no time in proceeding to Dublin, whither it was ascertained his father had gone, with the declared intention of meeting and accompanying him home. He arrived in town in the evening; and having previously learned that Dr. Danvers had been for some days in Dublin, he at once sought him at his usual lodgings, and found the old gentleman at his solitary "dish" of tea.

"My dear Charles," said he, greeting his young friend with earnest warmth, "I am rejoiced beyond measure to see you. Your father is in town, as you supposed; and I have just had a note from him, which has, I confess, not a little agitated me, referring, as it does, to a subject of painful and horrible interest—one with which, I suppose, you are familiar, but upon which I myself have never yet spoken fully to any person, excepting your father only."

"And pray, my dear sir, what is this topic?" inquired Charles, with marked interest.

"Read this note," answered the clergyman, placing one at the same time in his young visitor's hand.

Charles read as follows:—

"MY DEAR SIR,—I have a singular communication to make to you, but in the strictest privacy, with reference to a subject which merely to name, is to awaken feelings of doubt and horror—I mean the confession of Merton, with respect to the murder of Wynston Berkley. I will call upon you this evening after dark; for I have certain reasons for not caring to meet old acquaintances about town; and if you can afford me half-an-hour, I promise to complete my intended disclosure within that time. Let us be strictly private—this is my only proviso.
                              "Yours with much respect,
                              "RICHARD MARSTON."

"Your father has been sorely troubled in mind," said Dr.

Danvers, as soon as the young man had read this communication; "he has told me as much; it may be that the discovery he has now made may possibly have relieved him of certain galling anxieties. The fear that unjust suspicion should light upon himself, or those connected with him, has, I dare say, tormented him sorely. God grant, that as the providential unfolding of all the details of this mysterious crime comes about, he may be brought to recognise, in the just, terrible process, the hand of heaven. God grant, that at last his heart may be softened, and his spirit illuminated by the blessed influence he has so long and so sternly rejected."

As the old man thus spake—as if in symbolic answering to his prayer—a sudden glory from the setting sun streamed through the funereal pile of clouds which filled the western horizon, and flooded the chamber where they were.

After a silence, Charles Marston said, with some little embarrassment: "It may be a strange confession to make, though, indeed, hardly so to you—for you know but too well the gloomy reserve with which my father has uniformly treated me—that the exact nature of Merton's confession never reached my ears; and once or twice, when I approached the subject, in conversation with you, it seemed to me that the subject was one which, for some reason, it was painful to you to enter upon."

"And so it was, in truth, my young friend—so it was; for that confession left behind it many fearful doubts, proving, indeed, nothing but the one fact, that, *morally*, the wretched man was guilty of the murder."

Charles, urged by a feeling of the keenest interest, requested Dr. Danvers to detail to him the particulars of the dying man's narration.

"Willingly," answered Dr. Danvers, with a look of gloom, and heaving a profound sigh—"willingly, for you have now come to an age when you may safely be entrusted with secrets affecting your own family, and which, although, thank God, as I believe, they in no respect involve the honour of any one of its members, yet might deeply involve its peace and its security against the assaults of vague and horrible slander. Here, then, is the narrative: Merton, when he was conscious of the approach of death, qualified, by a circumstantial and detailed statement, the absolute confession of guilt which he had at first sullenly made. In this he declared that the guilt of design and intention only was his—that in the act itself he had been *anticipated*. He stated, that from the moment when Sir Wynston's servant had casually mentioned the circumstance of his master's usually sleeping with his watch and pocket-book under his pillow, the idea of robbing him had taken possession of his mind. With the idea of robbing him (under the peculiar circumstances, his servant sleeping in the apartment close by, and the slightest alarm being, in all probability, sufficient to call him to the spot) the idea of anticipating resistance by murder had associated itself. He had contended against these haunting and growing solicitations of Satan with an earnest and horrible agony. He had intended to leave his place, and fly from the mysterious temptation which he felt he wanted power to combat, but accident or fate prevented him. In a state of ghastly excitement he had, on the memorable night of Sir Wynston's murder, proceeded, as had afterwards appeared in evidence, by the back stair to the baronet's chamber; he had softly stolen into it, and proceeded to the bedside, with the weapon in his hand. He drew his breath for the decisive stroke, which was to bereave the (supposed) sleeping man of life, and when stretching his left hand under the clothes, it rested upon a dull, cold corpse, and, at the same moment, his right hand was immersed in a pool of blood. He dropped the knife, recoiled a pace or so, and a feeling of absolute terror for a moment froze him. With a painful effort, however, he again grasped with his hand to recover the weapon he had suffered to escape, and secured, as it afterwards turned out, not the knife with which he had meditated the commission of his crime, but the dagger which was afterwards found where he had concealed it. He was now fully alive to the horror of his situation; he was compromised as fully as if he had in very deed driven home the weapon which had let out the heart's blood of the dead sinner who was lying in the dark beside him. To be found under such circumstances, would convict him as surely as if fifty eyes had seen him strike the murderous blow. He had nothing now for it but flight; and in order to guard himself against the contingency of being surprised from the door opening upon the corridor, he bolted it; then groped under the murdered man's pillow, for the booty which had so fatally fascinated his imagination. Here he was disappointed. What further happened you already know."

Charles listened with breathless attention to this recital, and after a painful interval, said:—

"Then the actual murderer is, after all, unascertained. This is, indeed, horrible; it was very natural that my father should have felt the danger to which such a disclosure would have exposed the reputation of our family, yet I should have preferred encountering it, were it ten times as great, to the equivocal prudence of suppressing the truth with respect to a murder committed under my own roof."

"He has, however, it would seem, arrived at some new conclusions," said Dr. Danvers, "and is now prepared to throw some unanticipated light upon the whole transaction."

Even as they were talking, a knocking was heard at the hall-door, and after a brief and hurried consultation, it was agreed, that considering the strict condition of privacy attached to this visit by Mr. Marston himself, as well as his reserved and wayward temper, it might be better for Charles to avoid presenting himself to his father on this occasion. A few seconds afterwards the door opened, and Mr. Marston entered the apartment. It was now dark, and the servant, unbidden, placed candles upon the table. Without answering one word to Dr. Danvers's greeting, Marston sate down, as it seemed, in agitated abstraction. Removing his hat suddenly (for he had not even made this slight homage to the laws of courtesy), he looked round with a careworn, fiery eye, and a pale countenance, and said—

"We are quite alone, Dr. Danvers—no one anywhere near?"

Dr. Danvers assured him that all was secure.

After a long and agitated pause, Marston said—

"You remember Merton's confession. He admitted his intention to kill Berkley, but denied that he was the actual murderer. He spoke truth—no one knew it better than I; for I am the murderer."

Dr. Danvers was so shocked and overwhelmed that he was utterly unable to speak.

"Ay, sir, in point of law and of morals, literally and honestly, the MURDERER of Wynston Berkley. I am resolved you shall know it all. Make what use of it you will—I care for nothing now, but to get rid of the d_____d, unsustainable secret, and that is done. I did not intend to kill the scoundrel when I went to his room; but with the just feelings of exasperation with which I regarded him, it would have been wiser had I avoided the interview; and I meant to have done so. But his candle was burning; I saw the light through the door, and went in. It was his evil fortune to indulge in his old strain of sardonic impertinence. He provoked me; I struck him—he struck me again—and with his own dagger I stabbed him three times. I did not know what I had done—I could not believe it. I felt neither remorse nor sorrow—why should I?—but the thing was horrible, astounding. There he sate in the corner of his cushioned chair, with the old fiendish smile on still. Sir, I never thought that any human shape could look so dreadful. I don't know how long I stayed there, freezing with horror and detestation, and yet unable to take my eyes from the d_____d face. Did you see it in the coffin? Sir, there was a sneer of triumph on it that was diabolic and prophetic."

Marston was fearfully agitated as he spoke, and repeatedly wiped from his face the cold sweat that gathered there.

"I could not leave the room by the back stairs," he resumed, "for the valet slept in the intervening chamber. I felt such an appalled antipathy to the body that I could scarce muster courage to pass it. But, sir, I am not easily cowed—I mastered this repugnance in a few minutes—or, rather, I acted in spite of it, I knew not how—but instinctively it seemed to me that it was better to lay the body in the bed, than leave it where it was, shewing, as its position might, that the thing occurred in an altercation. So, sir, I raised it, and bore it softly across the room, and laid it in the bed; and, while I was carrying it, it swayed forward, the arms glided round my neck, and the head rested against my cheek—that *was* a parody upon a brotherly embrace!"

"I do not know at what moment it was, but some time when I was carrying Wynston, or laying him in the bed," continued Marston, who spoke rather like one pursuing a horrible reverie, than as a man relating facts to a listener, "I heard a light tread, and soft breathing, in the lobby. A thunder-clap would have stunned me less that minute. I moved softly, holding my breath, to the door. I believe, in moments of strong excitement, men hear more acutely than at other times; but I thought I heard the rustling of a gown, going *from* the door again. I waited—it ceased; I waited until all was quiet. I then extinguished the candle, and groped my way to the door; there was a faint degree of light in the corridor, and I thought I saw a head projected from the chamber-door next to the Frenchwoman's—Mademoiselle's. As I came on, it was softly withdrawn, and the door not quite noiselessly closed. I could not be absolutely certain, but I learned all afterward. And now, sir, you have the story of Sir Wynston's murder."

Doctor Danvers groaned in spirit, being wrung alike with fear and sorrow. With hands clasped, and head bowed down, in an exceeding bitter agony of soul, he murmured only the words of the Litany—"Lord, have mercy upon us; Christ, have mercy upon us; Lord, have mercy upon us."

Marston had recovered his usual lowering aspect and gloomy self-possession in a few moments, and was now standing erect and defiant before the humbled and afflicted minister of God. The contrast was terrible—almost sublime

Doctor Danvers resolved to keep this dreadful secret, at least for a time, to himself. He could not make up his mind to inflict upon those whom he loved so well as Charles and Rhoda the shame and agony of such a disclosure; yet he was sorely troubled—for his was a conflict of duty and mercy—of love and justice.

He told Charles Marston, when urged with earnest inquiry, that what he had heard that evening was intended solely for his own ear, and gently but peremptorily declined telling, at least until some future time, the substance of his father's communication.

Charles now felt it necessary to see his father, for the purpose of letting him know the substance of the evidence which had reached him, and also the events which had so recently occurred at Dunoran. Accordingly he proceeded, accompanied by Dr. Danvers, on the next morning, to the hotel where Marston had intimated his intention of passing the night.

On their inquiring for him in the hall, the porter appeared much perplexed and disturbed, and as they pressed him with questions, his answers became conflicting and mysterious. Mr. Marston was there—he had slept there last night; he could not say whether or not he was then in the house; but he knew that no one could be admitted to see him. He would, if the gentlemen wished it, send their cards to (not Mr. Marston, but) the *proprietor*: and finally, he concluded by begging that they would themselves see "the proprietor," and despatched a waiter to apprise him of the circumstances of the visit. There was something odd and even sinister in all this, which, along with the whispering and the curious glances of the waiters, who happened to hear the errand on which they came, inspired the two companions with vague and fearful misgivings which they did not care mutually to disclose.

In a few moments they were shown into a small sitting-room upstairs, where the proprietor, a fussy little gentleman, and apparently very uneasy and frightened, received them.

"We have called here to see Mr. Marston," said Dr. Danvers, "and the porter has referred us to you."

"Yes, sir, exactly—precisely so," answered the little man, fidgeting excessively, and, as it seemed, growing paler, every instant; "but—but, in fact, sir, there is—there has been—in short, have not you heard of the—the *accident*?" He wound up with a prodigious effort, and wiped his forehead when he had done.

"Pray, sir, be explicit; we are near friends of Mr.

Marston—in fact, sir, this is his son," said Dr. Danvers, pointing to Charles Marston; "and we are both uneasy at the strange mystery with which our inquiries have been met. Do, I entreat of you, say what has happened?"

"Why—why," hesitated the man, "I really—I would not for five hundred pounds it had happened in my house. The—the unhappy gentleman has, in short——" He glanced at Charles, as if afraid of the effect of the disclosure he was on the point of making, and then hurriedly said, "He is *dead*, sir; he was found dead in his room—this morning, at eight o'clock. I assure you I have not been myself ever since."

Charles Marston was so stunned and overcome by this sudden blow, that he was upon the point of fainting. Rallying, however, with a strong effort, he demanded to be conducted to the chamber where the body lay. The man assented, but hesitated on reaching the door, and whispered something in the ear of Dr. Danvers, who, as he heard it, raised his hands and eyes with a mute expression of horror, and turning to Charles, said—

"My dear young friend, remain where you are for a few moments; I will return to you immediately, and tell you whatever I have ascertained. You are in no condition for such a scene at present."

Charles, indeed, felt that the fact was so, and sick and giddy, suffered Dr. Danvers, with gentle compulsion, to force him into a seat.

In silence the venerable clergyman followed his conductor. With a palpitating heart he advanced to the bedside, and twice essayed to draw the curtain, and twice lost courage; but gathering resolution at last, he pulled the drapery aside, and beheld all he was to see again of Richard Marston. The bedclothes were drawn, so as nearly to cover the mouth; the eyes were open, and the face was hideously swollen.*

"There is the wound, sir," whispered the man, as with coarse officiousness he drew back the bedclothes from the throat of the corpse, and exhibited a frightful, yawning gash, as it seemed, nearly severing the head from the body. With sickening horror Dr. Danvers turned away from the awful spectacle. He covered his face in his hands, and it seemed to him as if a soft, solemn voice whispered in his ear the mystic words, "Whoso sheddeth man's blood, by man shall his blood be shed."

The hand which, but a few years before, had, unsuspected, consigned a fellow-mortal to the grave, had itself avenged the murder—Marston had perished by his own hand.

The concluding chapter in a novel is always brief, though seldom so short as the world would have it. In a tale like this, the "winding up" must be proportionably contracted. We have scarcely a claim to so many lines as the formal novelist may occupy pages, in the distribution of poetic justice, and the final grouping of his characters into that effective tableau upon which, at last, the curtain gracefully descends. We, too, may be all the briefer, inasmuch as the reader has doubtless anticipated the little we have to say. It amounts then to this:— Within two years after the fearful event which we have just recorded, a double alliance had drawn together, in nearer and dearer union, the inmates of Dunoran and Newton Park. Charles Marston had won and wed the fair Emily Howard. Rhoda had given her hand to young Mervyn. Of ulterior consequences we say nothing—the nursery is above our

---

* A common phenomenon in such cases; the severed muscles shrinking up into the face.

province. And now, at length, after this three months' journey through somewhat stern and gloomy scenery, in this long-deferred flood of golden sunshine we bid thee, gentle reader, a kind farewell.

References

THIS LIST OF REFERENCES is limited to works believed to be still in print that are reckoned as indispensable guides to the life and writings of Sheridan Le Fanu. Some pioneering earlier tracts, now no longer accessible, are referenced – with in several cases substantial excerpts offered – in the Crawford-Rockhill-Showers-edited text cited below.

E.F. Bleiler (ed.), *Best Ghost Stories of J.S. Le Fanu*
   (New York: Dover Publications, Inc., 1964)

E.F. Bleiler (ed.), *J.S. Le Fanu: Ghost Stories and Tales of Mystery*
   (New York: Dover Publications, Inc., 1975)

These two Dover collections, despite their publication dates, are regularly found second-hand and in reprint. They comprise almost all Le Fanu's ghost stories and mystery tales, including "The Mysterious Lodger", published anonymously in 1850, which M.R. James ascribed to Le Fanu's authorship, though doubted by Bleiler. The 1975 volume contains "The Evil Guest". Bleiler's introductions are readable and informative, if on some points challenged by later research.

Gary William Crawford, Jim Rochkill, Brian J. Showers (eds.),
   Reflections in a Glass Darkly (New York: Hippocampus Press, 2011)

A veritable treasure trove, invaluable for anyone truly concerned to form deeper understanding of the writer and his writing. Essays treating in depth of individual works will interest the academic as much as the general reader. Also included are extracts from earlier biographical and critical studies, contemporary reviews, obituary notices, and a detailed bibliography of original and secondary sources.

W.J. McCormack, *Sheridan Le Fanu and Victorian Ireland*
   (Oxford: Clarendon Press, 1980)

The definitive and so far only full-length biography. McCormack's study extends beyond biography and features a critical analysis of Le Fanu's writing set in the context of his life and times. He makes the case that the anonymous serialised novel *Loved and Lost* (1868-1869) can be accredited to Le Fanu. The author's access to and use of family papers enhance the strength of this magisterial work. McCormack's biography has gone through further editions, in 1991 and 1997.

Jim Rockhill (ed.), *J.S. Le Fanu: Schalken the Painter and Other Ghost Stories 1838-1861* (Ashcroft, British Columbia: Ash-Tree Press, 2002)

Jim Rockhill (ed.), *J.S. Le Fanu: The Haunted Baronet and Others—Ghost Stories 1861-1870* (Ashcroft, British Columbia: Ash-Tree Press, 2003)

Jim Rockhill (ed.), *J.S. Le Fanu: Mr. Justice Harbottle and Others —Ghost Stories 1870-1873* (Ashcroft, British Columbia: Ash-Tree Press, 2004)

These jacketed hardbacks from Ash-Tree Press are *de luxe* editions. Enriched by inclusion of both the Dublin University Magazine text of "Strange Event in the Life of Schalken the Painter" (1839) and its modified version "Schalken the Painter" from *Ghost Stories and Tales of Mystery* (1851), together with the rarely seen stories "Spalatro" (1843) and "Borrhomeo the Astronomer" (1862), rightly claiming prime place among the charms of these handsome texts are the extensive and insightful introductions by Jim Rockhill to each volume. Jim Rockhill's careful essays combine the not always linked strengths of erudition and empathy, and offer canny gleanings to the inner motivations of the author and his often psychically tormented ghost stories.

ACKNOWLEDGEMENTS

Nial O'Brien

Albert Power

Brian J Showers

Susan Waine